ACE HITS THE BIG TIME

Barbara Beasley Murphy
and
Judie Wolkoff

LAUREL-LEAF BOOKS bring together under a single imprint outstanding works of fiction and nonfiction particularly suitable for young adult readers, both in and out of the classroom. Charles F. Reasoner, Professor Emeritus of Children's Literature and Reading, New York University, is consultant to this series.

Published by
Dell Publishing
a division of
The Bantam Doubleday Dell Publishing Group, Inc.
666 Fifth Avenue
New York, New York 10103

To Stephen Murphy and Roger Wolkoff

ISBN: 0-440-90328-9

RL: 5.8
Reprinted by arrangement with Delacorte Press
Printed in the United States of America
December 1982
10 9

Dear Ace,

The membership committee of the Purple Falcons met and we'd like to ask you if you want to be a Falcon too. Yes or No. Circle one and return this here note to J.D. tomorrow at lunch. He's membership director.

We think you ought to join up with the Falcons so as not to get in with the wrong types.

Sincerely,
Freddy Cruz, Pres.

The wrong types? What were these guys? The note slipped right out of my hands onto the floor, and I quickly picked it up again. I had to reread it to see if I'd understood correctly. I gasped. I had. Me, a Falcon? Whew! What would they do to me if I circled *No*?

I thought of Guttenberg and the kids I knew there—Calvin Feckelworth, for instance. What would he say if he ever heard I'd joined up with a tough gang? The Feckelworths said they'd be visiting us in the city. Soon, they'd said. I almost laughed out loud picturing Calvin's shock. But if I told him I was a Falcon, he'd tell his mother, then she'd tell my mother. . . .

I didn't know what to do.

BARBARA BEASLEY MURPHY is the author of several books for young people. She lives in New Rochelle, New York.

JUDIE WOLKOFF has written several books for young people. She lives in Chappaqua, New York.

ONE

IT was weird. The face I was staring at was only half recognizable. Like it belonged in one of those before-and-after pictures in magazine ads where the two sides of a person's head don't match. In this case, however, the after side was *worse*. It was sickening!

"Would you hurry up in there?" my sister Nora yelled, pounding like crazy on the door. "You're not the only one who has to use the bathroom, y'know!"

I glanced in the mirror again and felt the knot in my stomach tighten. In forty-five minutes I was starting my first day at John F. Kennedy High with an eye that looked like it had stopped one of George Brett's line drives. *How could something like that happen overnight? How?* When I went to bed my eye was normal—if you could ever call anything about me "normal"—and this morning it was a mess. Red. Swollen. I could hardly see over the big yellow lump on the bottom lid—and I'm not exaggerating either. Inspecting it up close, you'd swear something like an egg yolk was about to ooze out of it.

"It's only a sty, Horace," Mom said when I came out of the bathroom for breakfast. "Keep your hand away from it and nobody will ever notice."

Ha, I thought. Unless sixteen hundred kids at JFK were blind as pea pods. Fat chance. I took a sip of the warm orange juice she handed me (the landlord forgot to tell us the refrigerator didn't work), then opened my eye wide and squeezed it shut a few times, hoping a little exercise would make the swelling go down. "Look, Ma," I said, "it's only the first day. I probably wouldn't miss much if I . . ."

She wasn't listening. She was standing just outside the kitchen with a broom in her hand looking at about a million boxes that were piled everywhere waiting to be unpacked. One lousy scene with me about not going to school was going to push her over the brink, start her crying. She'd been on the verge since Friday, the day we moved in.

Maybe things would have been different if we'd had a long, exciting move—say, from Istanbul to Hong Kong or something. But we hadn't. Ours was a short, rotten move—thirteen miles to be exact. All the way from Guttenberg, New Jersey, across the Hudson River to Manhattan, so my dad, a telephone repairman, wouldn't have to sweat the traffic anymore.

"I've had it," he announced about a month ago. "I'm finished . . . fizzled. Eighteen years of commuting is enough. We're moving to the city."

Within a week he'd signed a lease on the "hot tip" a guy on the job had given him. And the miracle, he said, was that the rent for this hot-tip apartment wasn't much more than what we were paying for our house in Guttenberg.

"Sorry you couldn't have seen it first, Flo," he told Mom the night he signed, "but I had to grab it fast. It would've been gone tomorrow."

We all pressed him about details, but he drew a blank on almost every question. "How should I know?" he snapped when Nora asked him if it was near a McDonald's. "I was in a hurry. Thirty people were lined up behind me begging to see it. It's on East Twenty-third Street, it's got three bedrooms, and it's on the top floor. What more can I tell you?"

Well, *I* can sure tell you something about it. This so-called "hot tip" he grabbed for us is the pits, and I mean The Pits. A four-floor walk-up to five rooms the size of gym lockers and every one of them with windows facing a gray brick wall. Except mine. It only has a vent.

The minute I walked inside the place I knew it was going to take me forever to adjust. But Nora, as usual, made herself at home right away. By Saturday she'd cased the neighborhood, found a McDonald's, met six other ten-year-old kids, and was back by noon to tell me I was going to get creamed by the Purple Falcons.

"The Purple *Falcons*?" I asked. "Who're they?"

"Oh, just the toughest gang at Kennedy—maybe even the toughest gang in the city," she said. "They mug old ladies and beat up any new kid they think looks funny. You're bound to get it, Horace."

That was two days ago. This morning she'd had a different opinion. When I walked out of the bathroom to let her in, she took one look at my eye and shook her head. "They're not just going to cream you, Horace —they're going to kill you."

I finished my warm orange juice and took another bite out of my soggy toast. Sixteen years plus four months was too young to die. "Would you please leave?" Mom said, taking away my plate. "You're going to be late." I was wondering if those were going to be her last words to her only son when she stuck something under my nose and added, "Here's your lunch."

"In *that*?" I yelled. "In a *clear* plastic bag? I don't want everyone knowing what I'm having. Don't we have any brown bags?"

Not one in the entire Pits. Only packing cartons and king-sized Macy's shopping bags. "You can use my old lunch box," Nora said. "I don't need it anymore—I got a new *Outer Space Adventure* one." She was feeling a little sorry for me, but I had to turn down her offer. What would the Purple Falcons do if they caught me carrying a bagel with cream cheese and a banana in a rusty Donald Duck lunch box?

I considered not taking any lunch at all, but then reconsidered, because my stomach can't make it more than three hours without food. Comes noon, I have to eat. I wanted to ask Mom for money to buy a sandwich, but she'd already told us that the move had brought us down to our last nickel.

It was either no lunch or my bagel and banana. I looked at them sitting on the counter, wondering what Nevada Culhane, the cool, cowboy hero-detective in the book I was reading, would do in my situation.

Nothing's too tricky to stump Nevada. In his last book
—*Devil's Paradise*—four cocaine dealers he'd been
tracking tried forcing him at gunpoint into a tank of
hungry barracudas, and he kept whistling "All the
Little Fishies Gotta Swim" while he figured out his
getaway. Somebody like that would sure as heck know
what to do if he didn't have a brown bag. I stuck my
jaw out and arched an eyebrow the way he does when
he's getting a clever idea. "Okay, Nev, baby," I said
to myself, "how're you gonna take your lunch to
school?" Then I answered, "You're gonna wear a jacket
and stuff it in your pockets."

I must've rummaged through a half dozen cartons
looking for my denim, but couldn't find it. The only
jackets I came up with were Dad's telephone company
winter parka (we were in the middle of a heat wave)
and the stupid-looking thing Uncle Jake had sent me
from Japan while he was in the merchant marines.

That still fit, so I popped back into the bathroom
for a quick peek at myself. Tall, skinny, and wearing
red satin with an embroidered dragon on my back. I
was a walking target, but at least the pockets were
deep enough so nobody could see my lunch. Too bad
there wasn't anything I could do with my eye. I tried
combing my hair down over it, but it just kept springing into a corkscrew curl between my eyebrows.

"Horace, *leave!*" Mom screamed from the kitchen.
"You've only got ten minutes—and *don't* forget your
registration card!"

I dragged myself away from the mirror and started
down the hall. Nora had left her door open, and as I

passed by I saw a pile of junk sitting at the foot of her
bed. Right on top was the disguise kit she got for
Christmas. My mind reeled as I stopped and stared at
it. What if I disguised myself? If I went to Kennedy
looking different from the way I usually do, maybe
nobody would recognize me when my sty was gone.

I darted in and took the lid off the box. Nora's
favorite disguise, the glasses with the hooked nose
attached to them, were in the first tray. They were
obviously too fake, and I was so nervous searching for
something better to wear, my hands were shaky. What
else was there? A big thumb that looked like it was
bleeding, vampire's teeth, a fake eyeball with a suction
cup on the back. I tried the eyeball but it only stuck
to my forehead.

"*Leave*, Horace!"

Just as I was about to drop the lid, I saw something
under the bleeding thumb. A black eyepatch. No suction cup or anything—just a simple, stretchy elastic
band that would fit any size head, including mine. I
snatched it out of the tray, grabbed my latest Nevada
Culhane book, *The Eighth Deadly Lair,* and dashed
for the door.

TWO

I GOT to Kennedy two minutes before the bell, but I didn't go in. I leaned against the wall of a candy store across the street and cased the joint. In my position, Nevada would've done the same thing. I opened my book, put it in front of my face, and looked over the top.

I watched and watched, but I didn't see anything much different from Guttenberg High. Other than being a little grubbier, the kids here looked about the same—jeans, T-shirts, big mouths. About half of them were dangling cigarettes from their lips. One was eating a foot-long pepperoni; ripping off big hunks of it with his back teeth. I had a feeling Nevada would spot things I was missing —the Purple Falcons, for example. Where were they hiding? I looked for unusual or odd things, but the pepperoni was the only thing I saw.

I wonder how long it takes to become a detective? I hope it's not something you're born with—a natural talent. If it is, then I'm a failure already. There sure

are a lot of things I never figured out before somebody else. I never knew my Uncle Jake was in the
slammer the year before he went into the wholesale
rice business. Old Nora knew all along. She told me
he evaded his income tax. Aunt Betty had said he was
in the hospital with the T.B. he got while he was in
the merchant marines. I'd believed her! I even sent
him a get-well card. Get smart, Stupid!

The patch was hot. I guess even your eye sweats
sometimes. I think that's normal—I hope so. Maybe
the reason Nevada sees more than other people is because he's not nervous. He doesn't get eye diseases
either. Right now, waiting to march through those
double gray doors across the street, I was nervous. I
glanced toward them again, but a maroon Cougar was
blocking my view. Move! . . . Move, I said to myself,
but the car stayed where it was until the driver and
the woman sitting next to him started pointing at me,
then they backed up next to the curb in front of the
candy store. Did they think they knew me? I'd swear
I'd never seen them before. They were still pointing,
excited, talking a mile a minute. I could tell by the
way their mouths were moving.

The woman began rolling down her window and I
made a dash for the street, then stopped dead in my
tracks when I looked over on the other side. Four guys
in black leather jackets had loomed up out of no-
where, heading for the school entrance. They must've
come from the subway while I was busy watching the
car. Twenty feet away I could hear their boots click
on the cement. Were they tough! One guy turned to

spit in the gutter and I read the silver nail-stud letters on his back—Purple Falcons!

I didn't know what to do. I didn't want to cross over, but the Cougar had pulled away from the curb and was easing up behind me in the middle of the street. "Hey, come here!" the driver shouted. He'd opened his door and I started thinking maybe he was going to force me into his car. You hear about things like that happening in New York.

The bell rang and I tore over to the other side of the street. By now the front walk was crowded with a thousand other kids and I moved right along with them, going inside. The halls smelled like old books, but the school looked pretty new. Waves of kids were branching off in different directions, and I turned with one group. Luckily, it was going the right way, and pretty soon I saw Room 107, my homeroom, according to the card the school had sent me. Teacher—Reggie Hatch.

A bunch of kids who were jammed in the doorway split to let me through. When they got a good look at me, heads whirled and I heard a chorus of "Son of a gun's," then a single "Get a load of *that!*"

I fought the urge to raise my hand to see if the patch was straight and my sty wasn't showing. I knew if I didn't act natural, they'd guess that I didn't always wear a patch. There was a seat halfway back next to the windows and I hurried over to it, looking around for the Falcons. Whew! None of them was there.

"Hi, I'm Raven Galvez—what's your name?" somebody said. The voice had a Spanish lilt to it. I took my hands out of my pockets and turned. Raven Galvez was sure a beautiful girl! I didn't know what to say. "Um—hello, Raven," I said finally.

"What's *your* name?" she asked again, but the bell rang. There was a lot of noise as everybody else came inside to take seats and the teacher slammed the door. He was straight and looked like John F. Kennedy, the man the school was named after. Only he was shorter and built like a boxer.

"Fill out these registration forms for class," he barked. "Anybody here doesn't belong in 107, Hatch's class, Kennedy High?"

Raven whispered, "He sounds like a grouch."

I gave her a glance out of my good eye and her eyelashes sort of fluttered when she smiled. I didn't have to be a detective to see that. Whew. She was unreal. Her skin looked like satin. Raven, I thought over and over.

Name. The form said. I wrote out Horace with my new Bic pen, but the ink wasn't flowing and the first letters didn't come out. What it said was: ace Hobart. ACE! Now why hadn't I thought of that *before*? It went so well with a patch. I looked over at Raven, who was writing her name in big, round letters with green ink. I cleared my throat. "Um, Raven?"

She looked up.

"My name's Ace. *Ace* Hobart."

She looked pleased and smiled, letting loose about three dimples in her cheeks. "Hi, Ace."

Hatch yelled at us and we went back to our forms. I didn't care. With a new name I was feeling like I'd just been let out of jail. Goodbye, Horace. Hello, Ace,

I thought. My heart was pounding—I knew my life was going to get better.

As much as I fought it, I felt the corners of my mouth turning up into what Nora calls one of my "stupid, dumb-jerk" grins. I didn't want Raven to see it, so I turned my head away from her, toward the window. I nearly died when I looked out and saw what was parked on the street—*that maroon Cougar*! Why were those people still hanging around? Were they *really* waiting to nab me?

I leaned closer to the shade, stretching my neck so I could see them better, and just when I got my nose to the window, the guy behind the wheel looked up. I quickly pulled my head back, but he'd already spotted me. Now he was pointing me out to the woman sitting on the other side of him. Why me? What had I done?

Forty-five minutes. It was the longest class I ever sat through. Most of the time I kept my head low, practically tucking it under my arm to hide it, but my neck kept cramping. Now and then I had to straighten it, and every time I glanced outside the maroon Cougar was still there. *Who are those people?*

"Where's your next class, Ace?" Raven asked when the bell rang.

I moved like lightning away from my desk, reading my registration card, and she followed me to the door. "Um, let's see," I said. "Epstein. Room 207. I think it's math."

"Darn."

I couldn't believe it. Raven looked beautiful when

she was pouting. And she really was pouting—like she was upset as anything that we weren't going to be together. "Then I go to Canfield," I said. "Room . . ."

"212?"

I nodded and she clutched my arm, smiling. "Me, too. Isn't that terrific? Maybe we can have lunch together afterward. I'd like you to meet some friends of mine."

"Yeah, sure," I said. I could feel her fingers on my arm even after we'd parted. I'd never been so happy. Lunch with Raven and her friends, who were probably six other girls as gorgeous as she was. If that was possible! My only worry was that I might look like an ape eating my banana. Maybe I'd just eat the bagel.

My head was in the clouds trying to find Room 207. Then I noticed the same strange thing that'd happened when I was trying to get to Hatch's class. Everyone was gaping at me. As I moved through the halls, some of the kids moved to the side to let me pass.

I went inside Room 207 and plopped myself in the first seat by the door without looking around. No more windows for me. But even by the door I couldn't concentrate. Epstein and math weren't enough to keep my mind off Raven Galvez—or the maroon Cougar either, for that matter.

Halfway through class I was sorry I hadn't sat by the window so I could keep tabs on those people. My curiosity was getting the best of me and I wanted to know if they'd moved their car. Darn. Why was I so jumpy? Maybe they weren't trying to nab me. Maybe the guy had just yelled, "Hey, come here!" so he could ask me a question. I had to start getting control of myself. So far there hadn't been much to get all worked up about—not even the Purple Falcons. I hadn't seen a single one of them since 8:59.

I felt a tap on the back rung of my chair and looked down. A big black leather boot with a heel thick enough to crunch a skull was sliding up the aisle, getting close to my foot. I got a tap on my ankle and somebody behind me went "*Psst.*"

I looked over my shoulder, twisting my head way around until I could see with my good eye. *A Falcon!* He was slumped down in his chair, holding up his hand, palm forward, the way Nora does when she plays Indian and says, "How?" Only this guy wasn't saying anything. I nodded—out of alarm more than anything—then turned around again.

I couldn't wait for lunch.

When it came eighty-seven minutes later, Raven and I were sitting next to each other in Canfield's class. She sighed when the bell rang and said, "Finally," then took me by the hand. "I can't wait to introduce you," she whispered as she steered me down the hall toward the front doors.

She wasn't the only one who couldn't wait. In all the years I'd lived in Guttenberg I'd never once had lunch with a girl, let alone a group of beautiful girls. I kept hoping the cream cheese in my bagel wouldn't stick to my front teeth.

"There they are," Raven said as we pushed through the front doors. "They're all waiting."

I took one look at the Purple Falcons standing on the

top step and nearly croaked. *Those* were Raven's friends? My first impulse was to run back into the school and hide somewhere, but I didn't have a chance. The Falcons crowded in on me like they were flies and I was flypaper. I took a deep breath, praying my knees wouldn't start clacking like a pair of castanets.

"Ace Hobart, this is Freddy Cruz." Raven's voice sounded far away as I looked at this brute, Freddy, standing in front of me.

"Ace, huh?"

I nodded. Freddy wasn't as tall as I was, but he was tall, and not skinny either. From the way he filled out his jacket I figured he'd been pumping iron since he was two months old.

"And this is J. D. Jackson," said Raven.

I glanced at the guy who'd tapped my ankle in Epstein's class. His Afro was close shaven with a crooked part running zigzag over the top. I'd never seen anything like it. This time when he gave me the "how" sign, his lips parted. No words came out, but I could see his teeth and I thought of the shark in *Jaws*.

"Ace—George Wyciewski." My eye shifted to the next guy. I was relieved to see that one of the Falcons was as scrawny as I was, but not for long. George looked meaner than any of them. I've read about eyes colder than steel bullets in my detective books, and he sure had them. I wished he'd stop staring at my patch. They all were.

"And last—but not least," said Raven, "Tony Vaccaro. Everybody calls him Slick." Slick. Beige hair, beige face, beige eyes without much expression in them. They sort of gave you the impression he had beige intelligence. He was the one who'd spit in the gutter.

The four Falcons. They stood there like they were waiting for me to say something. So far I'd just been nodding, and I knew I couldn't get away with that forever. Nevada, even in his worst scrapes, always managed to come up with a couple of sentences.

"So . . ." One word. The voice was mine, but I didn't recognize it. I'd always thought terrified people squeaked like high sopranos. But not me. I sounded like a hoarse foghorn.

"Where ya from, Ace?"

I looked at Freddy. "Guttenberg," said my hoarse foghorn.

He frowned, then nudged George. "Where's that, Georgio? Somewheres in Europe?"

George grunted something I couldn't understand and kept staring at my patch as if he thought it was going to rise like a stage curtain.

"C'mon, Ace," Freddy said as his iron hand clamped onto my elbow. "You come with us."

I thought of Nora's warning. "Oh? Where?" I asked, then wished I hadn't.

"Mario's Pizzeria. It's lunchtime, ain't it?"

The gang moved across the street with me in the center and Raven by my side. Mario's Pizzeria? I thought. Oh, sure. They were probably trying to trick me into going to their hangout so they could do whatever Nora heard they did to the new kids they thought looked funny.

There was no way I could escape them. I held my head high so I wouldn't look like a chicken, then swallowed hard, catching a glimpse of Raven out of the corner of my eye. I'd finally met the perfect girl and she'd set me up.

Raven Galvez was the Falcons' bait.

THREE

MARIO's was just around the corner from the candy store on Eighth Avenue. From the outside it looked like a legitimate eating place. I didn't know what to make of it. Maybe the Falcons had a private room in the back, but the business part seemed real. A guy in front was twirling dough. No boarded-up windows or anything. The door was wide open and I could see the place was jam-packed. I even recognized a few kids who'd been in my classes lined up at the counter.

"Ya wanna go in, or ya wanna eat outside?" Freddy asked me.

I shrugged. "It's up to you, Fred," I said, thinking Fred sounded more respectful than Freddy for a gang leader.

"Freddy," he corrected. "Fred's my old man." He looked around at everyone. "Outside then, okay? It ain't as hot."

He sniffed. Was that some kind of signal? J.D. clomped over to the window like he'd been given direct orders. The Falcons probably had signals for everything. So far I'd only caught one. I'd have to be on the alert for more.

"Six slices?" J.D. called to Freddy.

Freddy tossed his head back. Probably the signal for *yes*.

George wasn't staring at my patch anymore. Now his bullet eyes were fixed on my pockets. I shoved my hands farther into them, clenching my banana and bagel so he couldn't see them, but he already knew I had something in there. I expected him to start laughing, but he nudged Slick and whispered to him. Slick's beige face grew as long and serious as George's. Jeez, what'd they think I had? They backed off a bit, then George went full circle around me. When he came back, he was staring at my patch again. "Hey, Dragon . . ."

I looked over my shoulder to see who he meant, then I realized it was me. I'd almost forgotten what was embroidered on the back of my jacket. "Yeah, George?"

"A cop get you, Dragon?"

A cop? I didn't know what in the world he was talking about, so I kind of shrugged.

"Hurt much?" he asked.

He was driving at something, but it still beat me. I shrugged again. "Uhhh . . . nnn-yeah," I said. I thought that sounded sort of noncommittal.

J.D. was back with the pizza. Freddy handed me the first slice. Raven got the second. She held it on a square of wax paper and looked up at me with her big, double-crossing brown eyes. "Want to share a hydrant, Ace?"

"A hydrant?"

"Oh, I know it's not as classy as what you're used to," she said, "but it's better than standing." She pointed to a fire hydrant near the curb and motioned for me to follow her.

Just as I started across the sidewalk I heard a bunch of little kids screaming and laughing as they skipped down the street in our direction. One of them looked like . . . Oh, crap! It was Nora! What was she doing over here? Her school was on Tenth Avenue.

I dashed back to the entrance of Mario's and slammed my back against the side wall so she wouldn't see me. All I'd need was a big scene in front of the Falcons about how I'd stolen her eyepatch.

In a flash, Raven and the others formed a barricade to keep me hidden. "Someone trailing ya, man?" J.D. asked.

I thought fast. "A maroon car."

"Keep low and we'll cover ya," Freddy said as they all huddled closer together. "Don't talk!"

I squatted behind them and put my hand over my mouth. There was a pencil-size space between George's legs and I peeked through it in time to watch Nora and her friends pass by. Scared as rabbits. They nearly jumped out of their skins when Slick spit on the sidewalk in front of them.

She hadn't seen me!

I started breathing again when she disappeared around the corner and started to rise, but Freddy's hand crashed down on my shoulder and held me under. "Stay!" he hissed. "They're still there!"

Who was still there? I peeked between George's legs

again and saw the maroon Cougar coming down
Eighth Avenue. It was weaving around a truck, getting closer and closer to Mario's. "Eat yer pizzas and
act natural," Freddy commanded. I guessed he meant
me as well as everybody else, so I took a bite.

Nothing tastes worse than cold pizza, but I chewed
and chewed on mine until the car was swallowed up in
traffic. When I stood up, my knees were weak.

"Who are they? Big timers?" Slick asked, wiping his
mouth with something from his pocket.

Freddy glowered at him as he passed me an orange
soda. "Chill out! His business, dummy, not yours!"

"I got their license," said George. "Twenty-Two,
MMM from California. Figure that's some Mafia code?"

"His business!" Freddy repeated. Suddenly he
snapped his fingers. As if obeying a direct command,
the whole gang shot across the street. Nobody waited
for a light, of course, and a squealing van nearly
creamed me since I was on the end, tagging after
Raven.

"You're something else," she said when we reached
the curb on the other side. "You knew that maroon
car was coming before it even turned onto Eighth
Avenue. You got some kind of sixth sense or something,
Ace?"

"Oh, not really," I said.

"Nothing like false modesty!" she said in a mocking
tone. "So what's *wrong* with admitting you've got
something special?"

I didn't say anything. I have absolutely nothing
special to admit to except for a double-jointed pinky.

And anyway, we had to start running again to catch up with the Falcons. When we slowed down behind them at the next corner, Raven started in on me with her questions again. "Why're those people trailing you?" she asked.

"Beats me," I said.

"You won't admit to *anything*, will you?" She sounded really peeved, then she surprised me by taking my hand and doing this thing that girls in movies do. She cut her eyes at me and grinned—real slow. "Come on, Ace," she whispered. "You can tell me."

I felt something inside me melt, and I swear, if I'd known anything, I'd have talked. I really would've. "Honest, Raven," I said, tempted to cross my heart, "I'd never seen them before this morning. Really. I don't know who they are."

She practically threw my hand back at me. "Okay— *don't* trust me then!"

Back at school we all split up and went to our separate classes. Just knowing a few kids—even if they were the bad guys—made me feel better. I was just sorry I'd made Raven so mad.

French was my last period, and as I was walking in the door, a kid I'd never laid eyes on bumped me hard, on purpose, and said, "Here. Take this. It's from the Falcons." It was a note.

I got to my seat before I dared open it, keeping it hidden inside my notebook. What if it was full of threats and curses? My hands were so hot and clammy I had to wipe them on my jeans twice so the paper wouldn't dissolve. The message was short.

Dear Ace,

The membership committee of the Purple Falcons met and we'd like to ask you if you want to be a Falcon too. Yes or No. Circle one and return this here note to J.D. tomorrow at lunch. He's membership director.

We think you ought to join up with the Falcons so as not to get in with the wrong types.

Sincerely,
Freddy Cruz, Pres.

The wrong types? What were *these* guys? The note slipped right out of my hands onto the floor, and I quickly picked it up again. I had to reread it to see if I'd understood correctly. I gasped. I had. Me, a Falcon? Whew! What would they do to me if I circled No?

I thought of Guttenberg and the kids I knew there—Calvin Feckelworth, for instance. What would he say if he ever heard I'd joined up with a tough gang? The Feckelworths said they'd be visiting us in the city. Soon, they'd said. I almost laughed out loud picturing Calvin's shock. But if I told him I was a Falcon, he'd tell his mother, then she'd tell *my* mother. . . .

I didn't know what to do.

After school, there they were—the Falcons—waiting at the door. Right away they surrounded me on all sides. "Our messenger deliver what he was s'posed to?" Freddy asked.

"The note? Oh, yeah . . yeah . . . I got it," I said. "Uh, thanks."

They were all staring at me, waiting for an early answer I guessed. "Uh . . ." My throat was dry. I cleared it the way Slick does his every two seconds, then I heard my foghorn say, "What do you Falcons *do*, anyway?"

I think that kind of threw them. They all looked around to see if any kids were in earshot. Of course there weren't. I'd noticed this morning that nobody came within eight feet of the Falcons at any time.

"Hey, man—you *know*," J.D. said in a greasy way, heaving his shoulders and bopping around.

I was beginning to get an idea.

"Quit frazzling, J.D.!" George said. "This is serious."

J.D. sneered. "Just 'cause your body don't move right, George . . ." Raven, who'd just come out of the door, started bopping, or frazzling—whatever it was called—around back to him in the same rhythm, nodding her head so her long hair bounced.

"Hey, what do you guys do?" I asked again, thinking they hadn't heard me.

Slick slid his grubby hand up in the air. Freddy looked at the ground. There was a funny silence.

Then J.D. said, "Oh, a little hustling—uh, you know, mugging."

My hands began to sweat. They're always sweating.

"And some car jobs," Slick said, and spit. Watching him, I felt something thickening at the back of my throat and had to swallow hard to keep from imitating him. These Falcons were getting to me. I mean it.

"Want to come with us next time?" J.D. asked. He seemed a little uneasy about the offer. Maybe they thought I'd bungle everything. Raven tapped his arm.

To me it looked like she wanted him to be quiet, but then she started singing "Leave Me, Baby" and they did the frazzle again.

Freddy was quietly staring at me, watching my face the way a cabbie watches lights. I couldn't help admiring how he let the cords in his thick neck ripple now and then.

"Let me think about it," I said, waving my sweaty hand and starting off toward home. I was trying to walk in that slow one-sided gait that Nevada does. It gives people the impression that he's cool and gutsy, which he is, and which I'm not.

"Wait up, Ace," called Raven.

Suddenly she and the Falcons caught up with me and had me surrounded again.

"Where do you live, Ace?" Freddy asked.

That bothered me. If I told them the truth, they might come over. Mom would faint.

"Where do you live, Ace?" Slick said, parroting Freddy.

"Uh—you guys want to get in touch with me or something?" I asked.

Somebody said, "Yeah," but I don't know who. I was busy thinking fast.

"Well, uh—why don't you just leave me a message down at the uh—hotel?" I glanced down the block and saw the name Riviera. It was a hotel I'd noticed on my way to school this morning because a terrific-looking girl had come spinning out the door when I passed. She was the first person who'd seen me in my patch and, now that I thought of it, she'd sure done a double take. This patch must really do something to people.

"Where? What hotel?" asked George.

"The Riviera."

"Why can't ya say where ya live?" Slick said, sounding almost hurt. J.D. frowned at him as he rolled up the left leg of his jeans and Freddy told him to "Shut up."

To get off the subject, I asked J.D. why he was doing that to his jeans.

He looked up at me, grinning. "That's the way dudes on a Hundred Twenty-fifth Street do it."

"Well, I gotta go," I said, taking off, this time in the direction of the Riviera instead of home.

"See ya, man," the Falcons called.

I kept walking in Nevada's one-sided gait, counted to fifty, and then slowly turned my head to look back. The Falcons were gone. It was such a relief I blew out a lungful of air. I'd shaken those muggers at last, I thought. But less than a minute later I felt lonely—I missed them. Maybe they weren't so bad, I started to think. Then I realized I was going crazy.

The Riviera was wide open. Some guys in workclothes were replacing a slab of glass in the revolving door. The door was the only modern thing in the place. That's what they do in New York, Dad said. Stick on some newfangled thing so people will think the whole place is up to date.

The desk was antique and gave the trick away. It was one of those dark polished things with cubbyholes for letters behind it. Key rings were dangling

out of a few of them. When I stepped up there, I got
this feeling I was in a detective book. The Riviera was
the kind of place Nevada would go into when he
wanted info on somebody. I could picture him shuffling
through the lobby in his cowboy boots.

I coughed to get the clerk's attention.

He was a short guy with a wrinkled, striped shirt
and a sort of quilted-looking nose.

"Excuse me, sir," I said, then cleared my throat.
"Can I make a deal with you?"

"My name's Webber," he said, sliding his rump off
his stool. He didn't sound friendly or unfriendly.

"Mr. Webber, would you do me a favor? In return
I'll bring you a snack every day about this time." I
figured that was a good bribe because clerks probably
feel trapped behind their desks. It must be hard to
sneak out for a quick snack.

"What do you want me to do?" Now he sounded a
little bit friendly.

"Take messages for me. My name's Horace—Ace.
Ace Hobart. See. Here's the first snack. You get to try
it out before you decide." I unwrapped the bagel and
laid it on the counter in its waxed paper. The whipped
cream cheese was warm and oozing out the sides. Next
to it I put the banana.

"I don't know too many people in the city," I said,
"so it won't be a lot of messages."

Webber picked up the bagel and started to eat.
"What's your name again? I'll write it down," he said,
chewing with his mouth open.

A minute later business was settled and I was on

my way home. I couldn't wait to rip that darn patch off. It was driving me crazy, it was so itchy, but every time I lifted my hand to yank at it I thought I saw a Falcon lurking in a doorway.

Maybe I do have a sixth sense. Just as I was passing Gristede's Supermarket, who should be coming out the door but Raven, carrying a gallon jug of cider.

"Well, Ace! How about walking me home?"

It turned out she lived a block from my apartment building. Darn. I knew it. I'd be wearing this hot thing over my eye the rest of my life.

Outside her door, I handed her the jug I'd been carrying for her. "Thanks," she said, giving me a little hug. She'd brushed her arm against the pocket where I'd kept the bagel and she looked up at me, surprised. "You lose something?"

"Lose something?"

"Yeah, your brass knuckles—they're gone."

"Gone? Oh, ha ha—you mean my brass *knuckles*? Somebody ate them."

She must've laughed for five minutes when I said that. Really. She had no idea she was the one joking and I was the one being serious. "Bet you have another pair at home," she said, then laughed again.

I saw her looking at my other pocket. I had my hand in it, so I knew she couldn't tell it was empty. "George and Slick have a bet going about what you keep in that one," she said. "C'mon, tell me—I promise I won't tell them."

"Only if you tell me what they think it is," I said.

"I can't. I swore I wouldn't." She sighed. "Well, see

you tomorrow, Ace. I can't wait to hear what you tell the Falcons."

"Neither can I," I muttered. As I walked away, I thought, What *am* I going to tell them?

FOUR

Non compos mentis. If I don't remember another thing from my year of Latin at Guttenberg High, I sure remember that. *Non compos mentis!* i.e., out of it. Mentally deficient . . . i.e., ME! The words sure fit my state of mind when I got home after I left Raven.

Maybe it was a blessing I was so tuned out of what was going on in The Pits. Everyone was crabbing—Mom about the refrigerator, Dad about the subways, Nora about the Feckelworths. Actually, Nora wasn't just crabbing about the Feckelworths, she was screaming her head off, saying she'd rather *die* than have that jorky family visit us on Saturday. She gets rather dramatic at times.

As for Horace, alias Ace Hobart, all I could think about was the Falcons. Was I or wasn't I?—going to join them, that is.

The question kept me awake most of the night. Finally, around five in the morning, I decided I was. I'd join them. Nobody had asked me to be in anything since I left the Boy Scouts back in sixth grade. In an odd sort of way I was kind of touched by the offer. Really flattered. Me—a Purple Falcon. Incredible. Hadn't any of them noticed what a klutz I was? Everybody else did. Maybe they had and it didn't matter. Then again, maybe they hadn't and when they did it would matter. Lord.

I tossed and turned another hour. Muggings and car jobs. Me? How could *I* grab some old lady's pocketbook when I feel like a thief if I've got a book that's three days overdue at the library? And as far as car jobs are concerned—what *are* car jobs? Do you wash them, wax them, steal them, dynamite them, paint them, or strip them?

I got out of bed. My head ached. Everything has obstacles, I told myself. Some way or other, I'd get around mine. At least I hoped—no, not hoped, *prayed* —I would.

Nora was still sleeping. Ah, to have some peace and quiet in the bathroom for a change. I went in and closed the door. Then I saw myself in the mirror. Just when I was starting to get used to it, my sty had shrunk to the size of a small pimple. At first glance I had this strange feeling that part of my face was missing—like a nose or a chin. I sighed and put the patch in my pocket anyway. Sty or no sty, outside the Pits I had to go on wearing it.

It was only 6:30, but Mom was already up making lunches when I went out to the kitchen to pour my morning glass of warm orange juice. "Couldn't you sleep either?" she asked.

"Oh, I slept fine," I said. "Great. No problem at all. I'm really well rested."

"It's the vent! I just *know* it's the vent," she said. "You didn't sleep because there's not enough air circulating in your room!"

How can I mug if I can't even lie? The more I tried convincing her I'd never felt better, the more I convinced her I was a walking basket case.

"I'm fine," I kept repeating.

She gave me a sad little smile. "Things'll get better, Horace, I promise. Here's one improvement already." I looked at the brown paper bag on the counter. With all her worries—a bum refrigerator, no money, unpacking to do—she'd gone out of her way to get bags for my lunches. I didn't have the heart to tell her I was using my pockets. Or why.

"And I'm sorry you have to wear that awful red jacket," she told me when I was leaving. "I'll go through all the boxes today and see if I can find your denim."

"Aw, skip it, Ma," I said. "This isn't so bad. Honest. Besides, you've got a lot of things on your mind."

For a minute I thought she was going to cry. "You're such a good boy, Horace. You've always been such a good boy—so thoughtful." She swallowed hard and gave me a pat.

Why'd she have to tell me I was a good boy *this* morning? Why couldn't she have chosen a morning when I wasn't joining a gang?

"I try," I said.

She walked me to the door and handed me my lunch bag. "I hope you won't mind having a bagel and banana again. I'll get some salami for tomorrow."

I had no idea whether Webber liked salami, but I

couldn't tell her that. All I could do was explain that bagels and bananas were just what I wanted—that I'd really started to get used to them. "Besides," I said, "salami's expensive."

She was firm. "I know you like salami, Horace. And I'm getting you some!"

Without looking back, I could tell she was watching me go down the hall. I waited until I was halfway down the first flight of stairs and heard the door close before I whipped the patch out of my pocket. I put it on, wadded up the brown bag, stuffed the bagel and banana in my pockets, and flew down the rest of the stairs three at a time.

When I got to the Riviera, I was pooped. I'd run close to ten blocks in less than five minutes and I had to stand outside to catch my breath. Webber saw me from his desk and motioned for me to come inside. "You just had a caller," he said. "Wouldn't tell me his name. Tough-looking kid. You know—the type who walks like an ape. At first I thought it was a holdup."

"Did he have on a black leather jacket?"

Webber nodded. "That's right. With some kind of bird name on the back. Let me think now," he said, rolling his eyes. "Was it Vultures or was it Hawks?"

"Falcons maybe?"

"Yeah, that's it. It said Falcons."

"Did he ask you anything?"

"Not too much. He just wanted to know if anybody fitting your description had been in and I told him, 'Sir, we're not allowed to reveal that sort of information here. But if you care to leave a message . . .'"

"Did he?"

"Naw, he just walked away."

Probably Freddy, I thought. "Webber," I said, sticking out my hand, "you did a good job. Thanks. You'll have your bagel and ba—"

"Wait. Don't you want to hear about the other two?"

"The *other two*?"

"Yeah, a couple. Man and woman in their thirties, I'd guess. Real Hollywood-looking. You know—tan, big sunglasses. His shirt was all unbuttoned—"

Sunglasses! Now that I thought about it, those people in the maroon Cougar yesterday were wearing sunglasses. "Webber, did you notice the car they drove up in? Was it maroon?"

He shrugged. "Don't know whether I'd call it maroon or not. Maybe deep crimson. Or plum. Yeah, it was closer to plum. They parked it in front right after you left yesterday—said they'd seen you come in here."

I was getting panicked. It wasn't my imagination. Those people really were after me! "What'd you tell them?" I asked. "To leave a message?"

"I said you'd be in at three fifteen today. Why?" he asked as I moaned and buried my head in my hands. "Shouldn't I have? Are they going to do anything to you?"

"Yeah. Probably kill me."

"Sheez, I'm sorry. Look, I didn't know. Sheez—sheez, you can't trust anybody anymore, can you? Hey, look," he said, tapping my shoulder with his stubby finger, "if I did anything wrong, I'll split the ten dollars with you."

I looked up. *"What ten dollars?"*

"The ten they gave me. Two fives. Here's one—you take it." He slid it under my hand, then wrapped my fingers around it. "I mean it. It's yours."

I put the five in my pocket. Under the same circumstances, Nevada Culhane probably would've insisted on the whole ten, but I was too scared to get picky. "What am I gonna do, Webber?" I asked. "There's no way I can come in at three fifteen now."

He scratched his head. "Darn. I know. And I'm really hungry by then." He drummed his fingers on the desk and rolled his eyes up at the ceiling again. "Just leave it to Webber—he'll think of something," he said. Then his hand slammed flat. "I've got it! Let them come in at three fifteen. Why not? I'll worm a twenty out of them, then tell 'em you skipped town— moved to Miami in the middle of the night. Then you come in with the snack at three thirty, and we'll split the twenty. Fair?"

"Fair," I said as he shook my clammy hand. The guy was a genius. He really was.

If it had been hard concentrating in Hatch's class yesterday, it was impossible today. Raven was wearing a red blouse that matched her nails, her lipstick, and my jacket, and she told me she'd worn it for me. "To celebrate," she said when class was over.

How'd she know I was going to join the Falcons? I kept wondering all through Epstein's math class.

"A woman's instinct," she said when we were back together in Canfield's class.

Her long black hair fell in soft waves over her shoulders. Every now and then she'd brush a loose strand off her cheek and look over at me. "I can't wait to see their faces when you tell them—they really want you to be a Falcon, Ace."

I don't know how to explain it, but each time she smiled I'd hear Mom saying, "You're such a good boy, Horace." It was driving me nuts. Like some darned tape recorder playing over and over in my head.

"Well?" Freddy asked when Raven and I met everybody on the front steps at lunchtime.

"I'll join," I said, giving him my membership invitation with the *yes* circled on it.

J.D. yelled, "Whooo-wee," with a bop and Freddy told him to cool it, then smashed him in the rib cage with his elbow. J.D. doubled over in pain, still grinning. The others kept straight faces, but I could see from the way they were eyeing each other I'd given them the right answer.

So now I was a Falcon. Whew. Thinking about it made me feel giddy.

"Mario's?" I asked as we started down the steps in one tight unit. Freddy gave me the nod. "I'll buy," I said, remembering my five dollars.

"Slick buys," said Freddy. "Yer next Monday. We rotate."

Lunch went without a hitch. Nora and her friends didn't come sniffing around, and I was sure that after the scare the gang had given them yesterday they'd never leave the grounds of P.S. 60 again. One thing puzzled me, though. George and J.D. didn't stand around the hydrant, eating with the rest of us. J.D. ate at the curb about twenty feet up the street, and George ate at the curb about twenty feet down the street. Both of them were pacing nervously, like prowling leopards. "Aren't they talking?" I asked Freddy.

He grunted. "S'posed to keep their blinkers open. Nuttin' else."

"They're on the lookout," Raven whispered.

"For who? Cops?"

She shook her head. "The maroon car. Freddy said it was trailing you after school yesterday. That's why he and Slick followed you home."

Followed me home? They knew where I lived?

Raven must've been reading my mind. "With your sixth sense you didn't know that?" she asked, laughing. "They were a block behind you the whole way. This morning, too."

"Oh, I get it," I said, not getting anything. "That's why Freddy checked out the hotel before I went in— so I wouldn't walk into a trap?" The question was a shot in the dark, but I wanted her to think I had some grip on my life.

She nodded. "You're hot property, Ace. Nobody's gonna let you get shanghaied."

The Falcons—my guardian angels. It was unreal. None of them seemed to care *why* I was being trailed —only that I was. Respect for a guy's privacy. I liked that.

"Time," Freddy said. He snapped his fingers and my

bodyguards fell in around me like the ranks of a military platoon as we walked back to school.

Knowing I was hot property was sure helping me feel more secure. All during my afternoon classes I kept thinking how I was outfoxing my maroon shanghaiers. If they tried laying a hand on me, they were going to have to face the risk of being bruised and broken. Freddy and George were karate experts, Raven had told me. They'd had their brown belts for nearly a year, and now J.D. was working on his. Slick didn't need anything. Not with his phlegm act.

I guess I was a little too confident when I went to the hotel at 3:30. The maroon Cougar wasn't in front, so I pushed through the revolving doors, positive that Webber had already gotten rid of the people trailing me. I almost laughed. Suckers. They were probably hightailing it to Miami on their twenty-dollar lead.

"Hungry, Webber?" I asked as I strolled up to the desk.

"Beat it, kid! *Run*," he screamed. Then he ducked behind his stool.

From the wild look on his face, I knew he wasn't kidding. Somebody was waiting for me in the hotel! I whirled around. *The door . . . the door . . . where'd the door go? . . . I can't find it. . . .*

"Hey, Red Dragon," a woman shouted from the other side of the lobby.

I finally spotted the door behind me, ran to it, and just as I was shoving it to get outside it jammed. A man in sunglasses with a pink cigarette in his mouth had hopped into the glass section in front of mine, the woman from the lobby had hopped into the section on the opposite side, and they were trapping me in the center. My knees buckled and I could feel my heart skip.

"You're after the wrong person," I shrieked. "You don't want me—you want somebody else."

"No, it's you," the man said, tapping the glass between us. "We want you, Dragon."

He sounded just like Count Dracula. I swear he did. I rammed the door with my shoulder, but it wouldn't budge. My strength was fading. Was I passing out?

"Will you just *listen?*" the woman called from the section behind me. "We want you for a part in our movie."

My hands fell to my sides as I glanced back at her, watching her creamy coral lips move in her suntanned face. Then the two of them spun the door around till I was back in the lobby. I could see Webber's head slowly rising from behind his stool. "I'm sorry! I'm sorry! I tried warning you, but it was too late. I'll give you the whole twen—"

"Here's our card," the woman cut in. "We're François and Marilyn Maroon from the Maroon Movie Machine."

I stared at the card: MAROON MOVIE MACHINE in bold maroon print.

"Sorry we gave you such a scare," François said, flicking his pink cigarette. "But the minute we saw you yesterday, we knew you were our man. Are you interested?"

He was pure Hollywood, all right. Open, blue silk shirt, gold chain with one of those Italian doodads that looks like a twenty-four-karat wisdom tooth hanging from it. Some kind of phony accent. Probably California-French.

"It doesn't matter if you're not an actor," Marilyn went on. "We're not interested in professionals. We're after realism, and we think you can give it to us. All you have to do is play yourself"—she smiled—"for a hundred dollars a scene."

"What do you say?" asked François.

I said nothing. I couldn't.

Marilyn's eyebrows rose above the rims of her sunglasses. "Two hundred dollars a scene?"

I leaned against the couch cushion.

"Two fifty?"

I wiped my hands on my jeans. The Pits could sure use a new refrigerator. "Um . . . how many scenes do you have in mind?"

Marilyn's hand went to her chest. "My God, François! Did you hear that voice? *Bee*-u-tiful!" She took a deep breath and looked at me, saying, "Ahh," as if my foghorn had put her in ecstasy. "How many scenes?" she asked. "Eight, maybe nine. You tell him about them, François."

From the way he was smiling at her with narrowed eyes I could tell he thought she was overdoing it. So did I. "The name of the film is *Bound and Gagged*," he said, turning to me.

Bound and Gagged? They had me pinned to the couch, telling me about it. It was going to be a low-budget film (their third) about teenage violence—gangs, two stabbings, three muggings, an all-out shoot-'em-up with cops, a kid on the lam (me) who gets it in the end. Blood and gore all over the place. My stomach churned while I listened. I was going to have my throat slashed in a schoolyard and bleed to death under a basketball hoop.

"You'll be sensational!" said Marilyn. "Your whole body moves in an aggressive swagger. Every sinew of it!" She leaned closer, studying my face thoughtfully. "A year from now every kid in America will be imitating you—I guarantee it. Eyepatches will be selling like hotcakes. Every store in the country will be carrying them. Your name . . ." She stopped, and several of her well-manicured nails went to her cheek. "My God, François," she said. "We don't even know his name!"

"Hor . . . uh . . .Ace. Ace Hobart."

"Horasis Hobart. God! It's perfect—absolutely perfect."

"Just Ace," I said. "Ace Hobart."

"I kind of go for Horasis myself."

François's eyes narrowed again and Marilyn brushed some lint off her green skirt. "Well, we'll talk about names some other time. Right now we've got other things to discuss. That gang of hoods you hang out with—who are they?"

"The Falcons. Why?"

"We've been watching them and we've decided they're the raunchiest-looking gang we've seen in the city."

"Oh, but they're not really," I said, worried that the Maroons were going to tell me to keep away from them. "I mean they may look it, but—"

"Now, now," François said as he lit up another cigarette, yellow this time, "don't get so defensive, kid. We want them in the film, too. Two fifty a scene—same as you." He dug in his pocket and pulled out a crisp new fifty-dollar bill. "See this? It's yours if you persuade them."

I shrugged. How was I to know if the Falcons wanted to be imitated by every kid in America?

"Okay, kid. Two fifties. You're expensive."

"But worth it," Marilyn said as she wrote something down on a piece of paper. "Take this, Horasis. It's the address of the filming location—the little park just off Ninety-third at York Avenue. But you and your gang be *here* after school tomorrow, okay? We need to meet and get plans firmed. The first shooting's this Saturday."

"So soon? What about our lines? Don't we have to memorize them?"

"No lines. We don't work from a script. It takes away from the realism."

"Nothing to learn?"

"Trust us, okay?"

"Okay," I said.

Someone behind me coughed. "Can you use me?"

The three of us looked up at Webber.

FIVE

JUST BE myself, I thought at dinner. Old golden-voiced *Horasis* showing the folks out in Boise, Wichita, and Klamath Falls what a real, hard-core, tough-as-nails big-city hoodlum is all about. If the Maroons only knew . . .

How was I going to fake it through nine scenes? What made Marilyn Maroon think my body moved in an aggressive swagger? If I was known for anything back in Guttenberg, it was for the way I walked. Quack-Quack Hobart, they called me.

And realism. Were they serious?

"Horace!"

I looked at Dad down at the other end of the table.

"Huh? What—me? You talking to me?"

"No, I always call myself Horace!" he said, exploding. "Now, for the third time, would you wake up and pass those blinking creamed onions or am I going to have to walk across the table to get them myself?"

"Sorry," I said, passing the bowl to Nora, who passed it to Dad, then looked back at me the way she always does, like I'm some kind of oddity in the Guinness World Records Exhibit. "Sorry, I didn't hear you."

"Didn't hear me," he bellowed. "Do you ever hear anything?" He ladled a pile of onions onto his plate, then shook the serving spoon at me. "It's high time you outgrew that stupor you're always in. If you don't, you'll never survive in this jungle."

A month ago Guttenberg was the butt end of the world and Manhattan the center of life. Now it was a jungle.

"Oh, lay off him, Barney," Mom said, sighing. "Can't you see Horace isn't feeling well? He's had a low-grade infection all week. Look at his eye. It's still . . ."

"If you ask me," Nora piped in, "he's plain old love-sick, not sick-sick. I'll betcha anything he's daydreaming about that girl I saw him with yesterday."

Her hands flew in the air and came down again making a series of rippling curves. "Wooo-wooo! Sexxx-y!" she said, then whistled. "Didya kiss her, Horace?

"Aa-aaah! Aaa-aaah! Look at him blush," she cackled. "He's redder'n that stupid dragon thing he's been wearing. And don't deny it was *you*, Horace. I saw you meet her outside Gristede's. Me and my friend Kelly weren't more'n fifty feet behind you—I know your dumb walk." She looked at Mom and Dad, her eyes wide. "Can you bee-lieve a sexy girl could see anything in *him*?"

Neither of them answered, and she turned back to me, wrinkling her nose like a cat smelling a decayed fish. "I know *I* wouldn't."

"Nora, mind your own business and finish your dinner," Mom snapped. "Horace is . . ." She eyed me protectively. "He's, well . . . he's just not ready for a girl friend, is all."

"She's *not* my girl friend," I said. "She's just someone in a couple of my classes and I happened to bump into her."

"Boy, you can say that again!" Nora crowed. "When he says bump, he's not kidding. That girl had her arm locked in his and every time they took a step—wham! —one side of her bumped into one side of him. Better check, Horace. Your hip's probably black and blue."

"All right, that's enough, Nora," Dad said. "If Horace wants to tell us more, he will." He slapped butter on his piece of bread, eyeing me while he spread it with his knife. *"Well-ll . . . ?"*

I watched him coat his thumbnail. "There's nothing to tell," I said, swallowing a cold lump of meat loaf.

"Ohhh?" Mom's voice went up. "Is she a nice girl, Horace?"

"Very nice. Straight A student," I said, making up something I thought she'd like. "On the Kennedy honor roll, in fact."

"That's good," she said. "Very good." She and Dad were looking at me like I'd turned into a regular Don Juan. "If it's not prying, what's her name?" Mom asked.

"Ra—" Somehow Raven didn't seem like a name they'd believe was on an honor roll. "—chel," I finished. "Her name's Rachel."

"Pretty name."

"I suppose," I said, passing it off with a shrug. The

shrug came so naturally I felt like Freddy. Maybe some of his supercool was rubbing off on me. I shrugged again. Hard. For once I knew I really looked tough.

"*Now* what's the matter with him?" Dad asked Mom. "Is he developing a twitch?"

"Boy, do you pick 'em! A cop disguised as a cleaning lady. How can you watch such junk?" Nora said, coming into the living room with a bag of potato chips after dinner. I'd wanted to be alone. No chance. She was sprawling herself on the floor in front of me to watch TV.

"I'm not watching," I said. "I'm trying to think."

"Ha. *You* think? That's a joke."

Actually I was trying to figure out how I was going to persuade the Falcons to give up a life of crime to do a movie on a life of crime. Real sticky, that job. On a par with selling the Yankees the idea of going Little League. And now I had Nora . . .

I kept worrying that she was going to spout off about the eyepatch. She's never had an unexpressed thought or opinion in her whole life. That's why it struck me as very, very peculiar that she'd waited till tonight to blab about seeing me with Raven yesterday. Was she up to something?

She was sitting cross-legged with her red loose-leaf notebook balanced on her knees. I watched her suspiciously. "You know, Horace," she said as she pressed a couple of Flintstone stickers on the inside covers, "you're a total enigma."

I sat up straight. "Huh? Where'd you hear that? *Who* said so?" Now we were getting somewhere.

"Nobody—thought of it myself."

"Oh, sure you did! How'd you know what that means?"

"I'm ten, you twit. I wasn't born yesterday—I can think for myself, you know. And you *are* an enigma—"

"Ssshhh! Wait a minute. I want to hear this commercial," I said, thinking it might teach me a way to sell the Falcons on being in a movie.

"See what I mean!" Nora yelled. "Watching commercials! You're old enough to be in high school and have a sexy girl friend, but you're still a nincompoop . . . you're even a bigger nincompoop than *Calvin!*"

"Who?"

"Calvin, you nincompooper's nincompoop! That whole jerky family is coming here and it's all your fault!"

Calvin Feckelworth of Guttenberg? I'd forgotten. Saturday? Was that when Mom said they were visiting?

"Nora? When is it? When're—"

"I'm not staying in here to watch commercials with a nincompoop," she said, clomping out of the room with her notebook and potato chips.

I tried reconstructing last night's dinner-table battle scene. The one Mom and Nora had over the Feckelworths. Darn! I'd been so *non compos mentis*, worrying about joining the Falcons, I hadn't even listened. But now it was important. Saturday was the filming.

I couldn't bring that hawk-eyed baroque music freak Calvin on the movie set with me. The Falcons would laugh me off the streets if they thought he was my friend—which he isn't. And never was! Our mothers had just pushed us off on each other back in grade school. They'd thought two oddballs might equal one regular kid. But it'd never worked out.

"Wait," I called, running down the hall after Nora. "Are they still coming?"

"Who?" she said.

That gave me a moment of hope. "The Feckelworths? Are they coming this Saturday?"

"Don't know and I don't care. I already told Mom I'm not spending one single second with Fatso Hilda. And since *you* just sat there, letting *me* do all the squawking, you're getting stuck with *both* her and Calvin. Serves you right." She stuffed her mouth with a fistful of potato chips and looked nasty as anything chewing on them. "You've made your bed—now lie in it!" she said, quoting one of Dad's favorite lines.

Then she slammed her door in my face.

Both of them? Ugh. Calvin was one thing, but *Hilda?* She even made me grateful I had Nora for a sister.

"Hey, Mom?" I called.

There wasn't any answer, but I could hear her moving something around in the kitchen. When I went in there, I found her stooped over, digging through some packing foam at the bottom of a wooden crate.

"Uh—hey, Mom? Would you mind if we gave the Feckelworths a raincheck for Saturday?"

She came up out of the crate with a stack of dishes. "Remember these?" she said, peeling a newspaper off a blue-rimmed plate. "Jake sent them to us from Japan just before he—" She was going to say, "went in the

pen," but stopped herself in time and said, "went into
the wholesale rice business." Then she set the plates
on the counter and ducked back in the crate again.
"Now what were you asking about a raincheck?"

"If we could give one to the Feckelworths. Saturday's going to be a bad day for me."

"Why?" she asked, coming up with a stack of
wrapped cups. "What's wrong with Saturday? You got
a date with your friend Rachel?"

"*Who?* Oh—ha ha, you mean *R*achel. No, I don't
have a date with anybody. I was just going to look
around for a job. Part time, is all—nothing to interfere
with my homework . . ."

"Awww." She looked like she was feeling sorry for
me. "I'll bet I know why you want money . . ."

"Yeah?"

"Because I can't find your denim jacket—you want
to buy a new one. That's it, isn't it, Horace? The kids
at school are teasing you about that awful red thing."
She unwrapped the cups, letting the paper drop to the
floor.

"Oh, a little—I guess it makes me look kinda
strange," I said, staring at my feet. "None of the guys
in New York wear anything like it. Maybe in Japan—"

"Awww, Horace. You'll get a new denim—I'll see
that you do."

I watched her put down the cups and rub her back.
"Well, that's just it," I said quickly. "The guys around
here don't wear denim either. They wear leather."

"*Oh?*"

"Dark leather. Black mainly. Doesn't show dirt.

Wouldn't need washing," I added when I saw the frown on her face.

"Oh, come on, Horace—the only kids I ever see wearing black leather are hoodlums. Gangs on motorcycles. You don't want anyone getting the wrong impression, do you?—thinking you've joined up with a bad crowd?"

"Me? Oh, no—ha ha. Nobody around here'll think that, Ma. Maybe back in Guttenberg, but not here. All the nice kids at Kennedy wear leather—ask anybody. The school orchestra, cooking club—even the math team. They all got big leather jackets."

She handed me a stack of saucers to unwrap. "Well, if you want my opinion, I'd much rather see you spend your money on a good tweed blazer." She rubbed her back again. "But then, that's only *my* opinion."

"Then you don't care—I can get one?" I crumpled a newspaper into a ball and aimed it toward the garbage can, the way old J.D. pitches in his pizza crust. "And you'll tell the Feckelworths not *this* Saturday— some other time maybe?"

"Now wait a minute." She picked the ball off the toaster and dropped it into the garbage. "What's one thing got to do with the other?"

"I'm looking for a job. I can't drag Calvin around with me."

"So where's it written that Saturday's the only day you can look for a job? Look tomorrow. Look Friday. Look any day after school next week. Saturday you're seeing the Feckelworths!"

"But, Ma—"

"Horace!" she shouted suddenly, bent over the crate. "*Think!* Why is it *this* weekend, this *particular* weekend, that Frieda's offered to come over?"

Frieda is Calvin's mother and Mom's closest friend, but that was the only connection I could make.

"I'm thinking, I'm thinking," I said, wishing she'd stand up again.

In the same bent-over position she moved across the floor from the crate to the counter, carrying another load of plates. "Your dad's putting in overtime this weekend and Frieda's coming to help *me*—which is more than my own children have done. So the least you can do, while the two of us straighten up this place, is show Calvin and Hilda around the neighborhood. *With Nora.* She's going, too—and you're in charge, Horace!"

"Ma, would you stand up straight now?" I begged. Watching her was getting to me, making me want to bend over too.

She rubbed her back silently. "Then stop complaining about the Feckelworths."

Old tough Ace, alias Horace-the-pushover, ended up unpacking the rest of the crate, washing all seventy-six dishes, not including the platters, tea set, or the monkeypod bowls Uncle Jake had sent from the Philippines.

Then I took the garbage out to the landing.

When I fell in bed later I kept wondering if this double life I was leading was going to give me an ulcer. I hadn't figured out anything to say to the Falcons tomorrow. How was I going to break it to them about the movie? Hey, you guys, wanna be in a film and have your criminal abilities exposed? How about it, huh? Huh?

Oh, sure. They'd be so mad, they'd kick me out of the gang. Then what? Well, I've read enough papers. I know. Ex-gang members usually end up in the East River in a block of cement.

The thought made me break out in a cold sweat.

To humor myself, I tried being optimistic. Maybe they'd be crazy about the idea of a movie. But even that wouldn't free me of complications. I'd still be stuck with Calvin on Saturday. And Nora. And Hilda.

And the Maroons.

SIX

I STOPPED in at the Riviera Thursday morning and was surprised to see a grouchy-looking, withered old man at the desk instead of Webber. He handed me an envelope with a letter inside written in a spidery script. The letterhead said: RIVIERA HOTEL FOR NEW YORK'S ELITE.

Dear Dragon,

Hope this reaches you in the morning. I won't be at the desk when you get there, and Benson, the old priss taking my shift, can't be trusted. He's probably even read this.

The reason I'm writing is I wanted to tell you what's happening. First the good news. The Maroons gave me a part in the movie. I get to be a mugging victim. Now the bad news. I can't play it. Know why? Because the guy on regular night shift went into St. Vincent's emergency room a couple of hours ago. Appendectomy. Now everybody's shift is screwed up.

What gripes me is I'd been telling the dope not

to eat sunflower seeds. I warned him they'd stuff up his bowels. Think he'd listen? No. Every morning when I came in, shells were all over the floor. (Bet you can guess who had to sweep them out.)

Now he's paying for it. But where does that leave me? Taking his regular midnight shift on weekends, *plus* his 8 a.m. to 4 p.m. Saturday shift! You'd think Benson would switch with me on Saturday, wouldn't you? But oh, no, not him. (Make sure you don't leave him my snack. The priss doesn't deserve it.)

Well, old buddy Dragon, I guess I won't see you unless I find somebody to fill in for me. I've tried, but no luck so far. Why don't you come in some night to see me? If you can't, call. Here's my home phone number: 929-0010. (The hotel's number is at the top of this page.)

Aren't you glad your problems aren't big ones like mine?

Your buddy,
Webber

I could feel Benson watching me as I read, so I was careful not to let any expression cross my face. Nonchalantly I turned and went out through the door to go to school.

Without Raven around to distract me during math, I started thinking of ways Nevada Culhane would go about telling the Falcons about the movie. "Money speaketh" is one of his slogans. I knew I was on the right track. Then I remembered a line from *The Eighth Deadly Lair*. "Listen, Jocko," Nevada had said to a con man, "everybody's got his price. What's yours?" That inspired me.

Immediately I got to work and calculated that nine scenes times $250 would bring each of the Falcons $2,250! That sounded like speaking money to me. But was it going to be a good enough price for them? I had no idea how much they made mugging.

Over 2 G's. Was it worth risking my neck if they were insulted by the offer? Yeah, I had to admit it was. After all, I'd make $2,350—an extra hundred for playing middle man—if they agreed. $2,350! Nothing to sneeze at for someone who only earned $80 housesitting last summer. Of course I didn't even get to keep the whole $80. Forty of it was deducted because I broke a lamp.

At lunchtime Webber's note and the page of math calculations were in my pocket. I was about to face my moment of truth.

"Ssshhh!" Freddy said after we'd finished our pizzas. "The Ace here says he's got somethin' important to tell us."

Four heads turned and eight eyes were pinpointed on me like cannons on a warship. "Go on, Ace," Raven said, sashaying up to my side. "What's the big news you got? We're all listening—right, fellas?"

J.D. said, "Yeah, yeah," and everybody else nodded.

It was now or never. I shoved my hands deep inside my jacket pockets, then shifted my weight from one foot to the other. "I gotta job for us," said my foghorn.

George cocked his head to the side and arched one of his eyebrows up so high it looked like a tepee. "*Oh, yeah?*"

"Yeah," I answered.

He nudged Slick who nudged J.D., who then asked, "Yeah? Big one?"

"Yeah," I said. "Big one."

Slick's hands came out of his jacket pockets and one of them reached up to wipe his nose. It was the first time I'd noticed he had letters printed on the second joint of each finger. "What? A bank?" he asked.

"Uh-uh. A movie."

"*Movie?*" they said, their faces tense, giving each other the look.

Raven didn't say anything. She wasn't even smiling. Bad sign. Freddy glanced at her as if she could explain something I couldn't, then he shrugged—long and hard, letting his shoulders rotate in a big, wide circle. Nobody could mistake that for a twitch. "What's the plan, man? You figgerin' on us rippin' off the box office?"

"We're gonna star in the movie," I said, weaker than a man lost at sea. "But only *if you want*. You guys say no, we don't. Okay?" Just don't hit me, I was tempted to add.

None of them made a peep. A tractor-trailer truck rattled down Eighth Avenue and I could hear all eight wheels rumble over a manhole cover. Slick interlocked his lettered fingers. "C C A B A B A C," I read. Probably some kind of abbreviation for a gang motto. I listened to his knuckles crack. Sounded like he was attacking a bowl of walnuts.

"Heh heh. Ha ha. *Us?* . . . Starrin' in a *movie?*"

All of us stared at J.D. who was doubled over laughing, out of control.

Freddy grabbed him by the back of his jacket collar, standing him up straight. "Cool it, man, or I'll belt ya in the chop. Y'hear?" J.D. sobered right up, and Freddy let go of him. Then he looked back at me, face dead-pan as ever. "What's the gimmick, man?"

"Oh, no gimmick. No gimmick at all," I answered. "These people who're making the movie . . . you know, the ones in the maroon car? Well, it's them. They tracked me down, and it turns out they want all of us to be in it. Offered us some big money. *But?* Like I said before, you guys don't want to do it, we don't do it. Fair? No harm . . . ha ha . . . in saying no."

George's head was still cocked to the side. If I was any good at interpreting body language, then his always told me he hadn't taken to me a whole lot. "How much money, Dragon?"

"Two fifty a scene," I said. "Two *hundred* fifty, that is." I pulled out the page of calculations in my pocket and read it to them. "Comes to two thousand, two hundred and fifty each for nine scenes."

There was a long, low whistle. Freddy quietly slid the heel of his boot on the toe of J.D.'s boot and stomped on it like he was putting out a cigarette. J.D. winced and the whistle stopped dead in the air, then Freddy went on like nothing had happened. "This ain't no musical—no dancin' or singin' or none of that stuff?"

"Oh, no. Just your typical everyday violence," I said. "You don't even have to act. It's supposed to be about a tough gang and all the movie people want you to do is mug and fight."

J.D.'s eyes rolled and Slick coughed.

"Where do I fit in, Ace?" asked Raven. Now she was smiling.

"I don't know yet," I told her. "I didn't ask a lot of specific questions, because—well, I didn't know whether you'd want to be in it or not. Do you?" I asked, almost forgetting we weren't alone. "It's called *Bound and Gagged*. Will your mother mind?"

"Mind?" She rattled off a bunch of Spanish to Freddy, then threw back her head and laughed. It was the first time I'd ever seen Freddy amused by anything. He didn't laugh, actually. He sort of curled his lips and said "ha" a time or two, which for him seemed pretty close to hysteria.

"Don't worry about *my* mother, Ace," Raven said, finally, wiping away some mascara that had gotten smudged under one of her eyelids. "If she says anything at all, it'll be '*Que bonito dinero!*'"

It was all settled. The Falcons agreed to star in *Bound and Gagged*. The only two who seemed even a little hesitant were George and Slick. And they seemed more reluctant about the 3:15 meeting with the Maroons than revealing to the country what thugs they were.

When we met on the front steps to walk over to the Riviera together after school, Freddy was leaning against a concrete pillar just to the side of the gray doors, sipping a grape soda and having a private talk with them. "See this," I heard him saying as he tapped one of his nostrils. "Till it smells a rat there ain't no rat. Now shut up."

The three of them separated from their huddle as soon as they saw me with Raven and J.D. Both Slick and George were acting so sheepish they made me wonder what else had been going on. I eyed Freddy. He sure wasn't one to give things away.

"Hey, man, I'm dry," J.D. said when he saw Freddy's soda can. "Got any left?"

Freddy turned the can upside down to show it was empty, then mangled it. I knew he wasn't doing it to impress any of us. He doesn't have to. Pulverizing something just comes naturally to him. Sort of an automatic reflex, like swallowing.

"C'mon," he said, starting down the steps into the ten-foot clearing always made available to us by the kids leaving school. "Let's check it out." The rest of us followed him, pausing a few steps down while he stopped to give us some last-minute instructions for meeting the Maroons. "Ace here is the mouth. Any questions?" he asked, looking at everyone. Nobody said anything and he hurled his demolished can into a cement tree pot at the base of the steps. "Then what're we waitin' for? *Move!*"

As we headed for the Riviera, it suddenly came to me how I could fix things up for Webber on Saturday. At the same time, it would solve my problem of Calvin. Now if I could only bribe Nora into entertaining Hilda.

Ahead of me, Freddy kicked a rotten apple out of his path with one of his monstrous black boots. It flew up, twirling, hitting a street sign. Please, please, I thought, watching it land, splattering, in the gutter, don't let Freddy smell a rat.

SEVEN

"Yoo-hoo, fellas!" Marilyn was standing in front of the hotel waiting for us in some sort of brown leather getup dripping with fringe. The Falcons, Raven, and I crossed Twenty-third Street. "Yoo-hoo!" she called again.

"You know *her*?" Raven asked.

"Mmm," I admitted. "She's the director."

"*Director*?" George said.

"Waddya think she is, *estúpido*?" Freddy asked under his breath, "Daniel Boone?"

George frowned, muttering something I couldn't hear, then J.D. started in "heh-hehing" like he'd done at lunch. "Shut up, the both o' ya!" Freddy warned, giving each of them a sharp elbow in the ribs at the exact moment Marilyn started coming toward us, calling, "Hellooo, Horasis."

"Who's Horasis?" asked Raven.

I pretended I didn't hear and glanced at Slick, who was squirting Neo-Synephrine up his nose. Everything was going to be a disaster. I could feel it.

"Well, well, well-ll—just look at all of you," Marilyn gushed, extending her fringed arms like she was going to swoop us up. "The Falcons! Aren't you something now?" She backed up a step, taking us all in with an appreciative smile, then she winked at me. "Tell me, lovey," she said, twisting a silver Indian bracelet around her wrist, "did you tell your gang what I said about you yesterday?"

"About what, Mrs. Maroo—"

"Marilyn."

"Marilyn," I repeated, hoping she wasn't going to bring up my aggressive swagger.

"Why, that gorgeous voice of yours, of course!"

"Ay, *caramba*!" whispered Raven, looking furious.

Marilyn squeezed in between me and Raven. I was cornered. "Fellas," she said, straightening my eyepatch, "a year from now your friend Horasis here is going to be the rage of America. And so are *you*," she added dramatically, sweeping her hand to include everyone, even Raven. "You'll be *les legendes du temps*."

"What's that?" Freddy asked.

"Legends of your time."

Everybody was stunned silent. They looked the way people do when their pictures are taken right after they've been told they won the lottery. "But meanwhile," Marilyn said, clasping her hands, "we've got a lot of things to talk over. And François's in the lobby waiting to meet you."

She whirled around and headed for the revolving doors. The rest of us just stood there looking at each other. "Ya heard the lady. Move!" ordered Freddy.

"Well, well, well! The famous Falcons!" François

exclaimed as we spun into the lobby two at a time.
He did a double take when he saw Raven. "And who is
this?" he asked, looking her up and down and smiling
in a way I didn't like.

"Raven," I said, stepping between them.

"Clever of the Falcons to have such a beautiful
bird!" he said, laughing at his own joke.

Marilyn looked exasperated, going "Uh-hmmm" several times before she caught his attention. "Why don't
we sit down and have the fellas introduce themselves,
dear?" she said, motioning for us to follow her to the
couches. Then, as an afterthought, she looked back at
Raven, adding, "You too, if you want," making it sound
like "You too, if you have to, pest."

"*Sí, tortuga grande*," Raven muttered to herself.

Marilyn's ears perked right up and she turned
around again. "Does your friend speak English,
Horasis?"

I nodded.

"Oh," she said, flashing two rows of perfectly capped
teeth. "Then I suppose she's interested in a small
part?"

"Tell her yes," Raven told me, matching smiles with
Marilyn.

"Yes," I repeated. "Yes, she is."

"Yes? Well, perhaps François can find something
suitable."

"Perhaps François can find something suitable," I
repeated to Raven.

"I know. I heard, *Horasis, lovey*," she said sarcasti-
cally. What had come over the two of them? I suddenly
thought of Nevada Culhane—first time all day, actu-

ally—and wondered how he could juggle a whole string of women, keeping every one of them crazy about him. Where'd I go wrong?

François was offering his pastel cigarettes, getting refusals right down the line. "Pfew—pink?" "Fruit weeds?" "Ya gotta be kiddin'." Freddy sat down first, plopping himself in the center of one of the couches, then he stuck his boots up on the coffee table, which got him a sour look from Benson, who was sitting on Webber's stool pretending to read a newspaper. Poor Webber. He'd be broken-hearted if he knew we were meeting without him. My hand felt the note in my pocket. I'd call him tonight for sure.

"Well, fellas," Marilyn began after we'd all squeezed onto the couches, "now that we're assembled, why don't you tell us your names and a little bit about yourselves?" She had a pad and suddenly looked very businesslike.

There was an awkward silence and she looked at J.D. "Starting with you."

"Heh-heh. Heh-heh, heh-heh."

"Phfew," went George next to me. "Listen to that. Can't he even—"

"Tell her it's J.D.," Freddy coached. "J.D. Jackson, remember?"

"I'm Jackson Donald Jackson and I'm from New York and, heh-heh, my old man used to be a boxer—"

Freddy nudged Slick, who was sitting between him and J.D. "Tony Vaccaro's the name. But the guys call me Slick—um—because of a habit of mine." He cleared his throat. "You think I ought to tell what it is?" he whispered to Freddy.

"Naw. Skip it."

Slick shrugged, then looked back at Marilyn. "I got my nose and jaw broke last year. And I got a cousin who's a jockey. And—anything else you want to know?"

"That's fine," Marilyn said, eager to get on to Freddy. "And how about you?"

"The name's Freddy. Short for Frederico Emanuel Cruz. I was born in the D.R. but I ain't been back there since I was nine months. Also I gotta brown belt in karate."

"And a lot of nice muscles," said Marilyn, looking over at the couch where the rest of us were sitting. "Horasis?" she said, skipping Raven.

François blew out a cloud of smoke. "Wait! Hold it, darling," he said, putting his briefcase on the floor. "The girl's next."

Raven crossed her graceful legs and sat up tall. "I'm Raven Galvez, Freddy Cruz's second cousin," she said in that knock-'em-dead way of hers. "I'm a quarter Cherokee Indian and I've got a scholarship at the Spanish-American Cultural Institute for Performing Arts."

"Oh?" asked François. "Studying what?"

"Flamenco."

"*Psst!*" went Freddy, making some kind of signal.

Raven blushed and looked down at her fingers. "I don't know whether this is important or not, but Freddy thinks I should tell you. I'm on the honor roll at Kennedy."

"You wha—" I blurted out.

"Does it matter, lovey?" she snipped.

"Splendid, splendid!" bubbled François. "A scholar."

"Horasis?"

"Huh?" I looked up at Marilyn perched on the arm of the other couch, fiddling with the fringe on her sleeve. "What?"

"Let's have a few words about you."

"Well—" I watched Raven turn her head away. She really hated me. "I just moved here from Guttenberg," I said, then paused, trying to think of something that might get me on her good side again. "And I used to study tap dancing. But I don't anymore," I added quickly seeing the kind of look Freddy was giving me. "And I've got an uncle who was in the slammer. His name's Jake. Big gangster. Big, big gangster. We're real close."

"Tell the story of your eye," said George.

"My eye? Oh, ha ha—you mean my *eye*. Aww," I said with a shrug, "you don't want to hear about that."

Raven's face softened and she seemed interested again, maybe even a little sympathetic.

"And *you*?"

George folded his arms and sniffed. His cold steely eyes, I'm happy to say, made even Marilyn uncomfortable. "I'm George Wyciewski," he said slowly and deliberately, a slight snicker on his face.

I watched Marilyn nervously rake her fingers through her hair. "Yes?" she said, breaking the word into two syllables.

"So what I want to know is why're you dressed up like Grizzly Adams. Aren't you supposed to be a director or something?"

Marilyn's dark eyes flew open, all fiery. "I'll have

you know that *this*," she said sharply, caressing the fringe, "is from Bergdorf Goodman. And what do *you* know about directors anyway? Ever seen one?" she spit out, tough as leather herself.

George nodded. "Yeah, a few. Kubrick, De Palma, Benton, Coppola, Scorsese——" he said, coolly ticking off names like he was reciting the alphabet. Everybody but Marilyn broke up, laughing. Even Freddy couldn't stop grinning, it was so unexpected. "But don't get me wrong," George added as he slumped back against his couch cushion. "I only seen pictures of them. I read *People* and *Time*."

George's answer really caught Marilyn off guard. She was so mad I was afraid we'd have to kiss our movie careers goodbye. Fortunately, François broke in, more tolerant. "This group session has given me a very interesting insight into your complex personalities," he said, lighting a cigarette the color of celery. "Without reservation, I predict your performances will be the tour de force in giving *Bound and Gagged* a fifth dimension." He caught Marilyn's eye and smiled. "And I'm sure Marilyn agrees. Don't you, darling?"

"Yes. Certainly," she said, twisting her bracelet.

No one objected. Maybe because we weren't sure what he was talking about. Then he proceeded to give us a blow-by-blow account of all our scenes—the knifings, the muggings, the gang rumble on the dock, my ghastly bloody ending under the basketball hoop, etc., etc., which didn't faze anybody in the least. Including Raven, I might add.

When François was finished, George asked a lot of probing questions about our last scene in the movie.

My first reaction was he couldn't wait to see my
throat slit. Look at him, I thought. Just listening to
the details is giving him a thrill.

Then I realized I was wrong. Old, smart George had
figured out way ahead of the rest of us that our scenes
were only a part of the movie. A third to be exact. The
other two-thirds, François finally admitted after a lot
of pressure from George, had already been shot without us.

"Two-thirds?" somebody hollered.

"Without us?"

"Hey! Waddya mean—who done 'em and where?"
said Slick.

The questions were coming so fast I couldn't tell
who was asking what. It seemed like the beginning of
a revolution, not a typical business meeting.

"It doesn't matter—doesn't matter." Marilyn's voice
rang over the clamor. "You'll steal the whole film anyway. You're in the New York sequences and the New
York sequences are the essence of the entire story!"

"*New York sequences?*" Everybody looked at everybody else.

"I thought you said we was the stars," said Freddy.

"You are," said Marilyn.

"Now hold it, lady!" George's eyes drilled right
through her. "Don't go hanging placebos on us. Either
you level or we're walking out. You got that?"

"And just *how* am I supposed to level?" she shot
back.

George leaned forward. "For instance, contracts.
When're we gonna—"

"Glad you brought that up," François cut in. He opened his briefcase and pulled out some papers, holding them in his hands like playing cards. "Copies for you. Copies for us. And the originals go to our office in California. Now if you'd like me to take a minute to explain—"

"We read," said George. "Including *fine* print. Just pass them out."

Each of us got a copy, George zooming through his like he had a doctorate in speed-reading. "Does it meet with everyone's approval?" Marilyn asked, setting a gold fountain pen on the table.

George flipped back to the second page, rereading the complicated middle section I was still struggling with, then looked up at her. "I got two questions. And no window dressing this time or we don't sign."

"Questions about *what*?" she said, like she wanted to choke him.

"Well, everything's all set up with the mayor's office so we can start shooting this weekend, right?"

"Right."

"Then why'd you wait till now to find your actors? Doesn't sound professional."

"Wait—let me tell him," François said while Marilyn took a deep breath. "We had a gang—*actors*, that is, a *mar*velous group of actors—coming in from Chicago. The leader, the one Horasis is replacing, cracked up his motorcycle this weekend and—"

"Why Chicago?" blurted out J.D. "Whatsa matter with New York?"

"Did he die?" asked Slick.

François rubbed between his eyes like he had a splitting headache. "No, no, he didn't die. He broke his leg—had a compound fracture and needed an operation for a steel pin. But the others wouldn't come here without him, and the reason we were getting them from Chicago," he said, his voice climbing with each word, "is because *that's* where our talent scouts found them last spring."

"They shoulda known we're tougher in New York," said Freddy.

"Thanks," François said to Raven, who handed him a tiny tin of aspirins from her pocket.

"So they left you high and dry," said George, "and you need us as last-minute stand-ins."

Marilyn forced a smile. "Of course, if Talent had seen you fellas first, *you* would've been picked."

"Cut the soap," he said. "We'll sign. We just wanted the facts."

François sank into his chair, sighing. "Good, good. The bottom line on the second page. Pen's on the table."

"And if you don't mind," said Marilyn, "can we skip the rest of the movie plot for now? I'll finish telling you on Saturday."

EIGHT

IF THE Falcons were having second thoughts about being actors in a movie, they sure weren't showing it by the time we signed our contracts.

"Now I can have that triple martini," Marilyn said, flushed and elated. Then she handed everybody a card with the address of the set location, same as she'd given me the day before. "Here's yours, lovey," she whispered as she discreetly slipped something into my pocket. "Two fifty-dollar bills under your banana."

Except for J.D., no one heard her. He heh-heh'd a few times, then said, "Don't get trigger happy with the banana in your pocket, man," nudging me.

"Don't worry," I joked back, patting my other pocket. "I won't even pull the pin out of my, ha ha, bagel."

I don't know why I suddenly felt so free to fool around with J.D. Maybe it was because his nervous laugh was as bad as mine. I'm not sure. But, whatever it was, he thought the bagel bit was a riot. "Man, someday you're gonna be the white man's Bill Cosby."

Suddenly everybody looked over at the desk, where

Benson was lacing into some guy who was an hour late for the four o'clock shift. Both Marilyn and I thought of Webber at the same time. "By the way, Horasis," she said, stopping me as all of us Falcons and Raven were about to leave, "what's happening with your friend Saturday? Scrooge over there says he's got to work here all day."

"Benson? Aw, he doesn't know anything," I said. "Webber'll make it to the shooting on time. Some guy from New Jersey's coming in to replace him."

Just as we all got out the door, the crosstown bus pulled up in front of the Riviera. The Falcons made a dash, sweeping me up with them. We all crowded inside before it took off, even though the driver tried closing the doors on us as soon as we got to the steps.

Freddy's oxen shoulders helped us. He smashed against the doors till they gave and we flooded past the screaming red-faced driver, flashing our student bus passes.

"What's happening? Ain't you s'posed to go uptown?" Freddy asked Slick when we'd settled in the long row of seats in the rear.

Slick grinned. "Yeah, but I wanna ride with you guys a ways—rap awhile. You know—the movie. You gonna get haircuts?"

Freddy looked at me. "Waddya think, Ace?"

"I had one last week." My mom insisted on it, but I didn't tell him that.

"I'm not," said George.

"Me neither," said J.D.

Freddy felt the tufts of thick black hair at the nape of his neck. "I wasn't figgerin' on one till Thanksgivin'."

"Yeah, mine oughtta go about that long too," Slick said, springing to his feet; he got off at the first stop to transfer uptown.

Within three stops, Raven and I were alone. "Sorry I was so rotten to you at the hotel," she said, putting her hand on my leg.

I looked at it. A perfect hand. Smooth, soft—delicate. But what was I supposed to do? Hold it? "That's okay," I said, doing nothing.

"Ohh, you're still mad, Ace. I can tell," she said, taking her perfect hand back to her own lap. "But I couldn't help the way I was acting. I'm emotional—high strung. Especially when I like somebody a lot . . . and I've never liked anybody as much as I like you."

I felt my throat close. "Thanks," I said.

"*Thanks?* That's *all* you have to say?"

"Well—uh, I—thanks *very much?*"

Soon as I said it I knew it was dumb. But I didn't expect her to laugh at me. Out loud.

"Ohhh, Ace," she said after she'd laughed and I'd wished I'd been born mute as well as stupid, "you really *are* the funniest person I've ever met."

The bus had come to our stop and she took my hand without waiting for me to take hers. "Come on, walk me home—please?" she said as we got off.

"Sure," I said squeezing her hand just enough to let her know she didn't have hold of a dead fish but not enough to let her think I was a sex fiend or anything.

There was a long line of people waiting to get on at the bus stop. For a minute I lost her. "Here I am," she said, coming around from behind me and taking my hand again. "Isn't New York awful at this hour?"

I nodded.

She smiled. "You know what? Sometimes I get the impression that all the people who ever lived get resurrected every day at five o'clock. And then they're dumped on the sidewalks of Manhattan—in horrible dispositions."

She looked so pretty with the wind blowing her hair past her cheek like a black silk flag, I didn't notice a big burly man wearing a hard hat until he slammed into me. "Why don't ya watch where you're movin', kid," he hollered.

I looked at Raven. "I see what you mean."

"Do you? Do you really, Ace?"

"Yeah—even the Neanderthals get resurrected."

She squeezed my hand. It was getting a little numb. "I knew you were different—from the minute I laid eyes on you. Most of the other guys I've known—oh, not the Falcons, they're like brothers to me, the other ones—they've always fed me corny lines. You know, junk like *silken hair* and chocolate eyes! They didn't care what I was thinking." We were in front of her building and she dug into her pocketbook for a key. "Want to come up?"

"Uh—I—darn! It's too late," I said quickly. I didn't know what she expected and I was half afraid to find out.

"The twins can't wait to see you."

"Who're the twins?"

"Carlos and Sylvia. They're six. Real characters.

What about you? Do you have any brothers or sisters, Ace?"

"One."

"Which?"

"A sister. Nora. She's a total enigma."

Raven laughed. "For some reason I see you as an only child—somebody who sprang out of a seashell, sort of—"

"That's funny," I said, stumped for something else to say. Then my foghorn said, "I sort of pictured you the same way, Raven."

She smiled and stuck the key in the lock. "Promise you'll come tomorrow?"

"I'll try!" I said, and turned, floating down the street.

Probably I would have forgotten about everybody in the world except Raven, if I hadn't passed a pay phone. I stopped, trying to think of who I'd been meaning to call. Then I remembered the note in my pocket. Webber. I couldn't do it at home—it'd be too complicated.

I didn't have any change, just the two fifties Marilyn had given me. The guy in the corner deli was a crab and refused to change them. So although I wasn't really hungry, I bought a bagel with cream cheese and went back to the pay phone. Webber had been asleep and sounded groggy, but he recognized my voice right away.

"Hey, One-eyed Wonder! How ya doing, kid? I was hoping you'd call. Isn't this the pits—the night shift rupturing his appendix on me? Don't know what I'm going to do about Saturday."

"Don't worry, Webber, you'll make it," I told him. "I've got a guy coming from New Jersey to take over the desk for you."

"What? You what? Say that again. You got me a replacement?" He sounded so thrilled, I could picture his pudgy body quivering with excitement. "Who? You're not putting me on now—you really got somebody?"

"I really did. Nice kid. Name's Calvin Feckelworth. I'll bring him over to the hotel soon as he gets here Saturday. Okay?"

Webber was choked up. "Thanks, kid. I mean it. This is the nicest thing anybody's ever done for me. I mean it. Nobody cares much these days for an old guy living all alone, no family and all. I'm not gonna forget it. I mean it."

I felt good going home. The Maroons were happy, the Falcons were happy, Raven was happy, Webber was happy, I was happy. I waved to a woman in a black shawl who was selling beaded slippers from a suitcase in front of my doorway.

"*Pobre tuerto,*" she said, pointing to my eye.

"It's nothing—*nada,*" I said, flying up the steps. "All's right with the world and all the creatures who inhabit it." My own words had such a ring to them I wondered if I'd heard them before. I didn't think so. Maybe I had a poet sleeping inside me.

My eyepatch! I slipped it into my pocket and opened our door.

"You'll never guess the good news, Horace," Nora said as I came inside. "Calvin has a cold and the Feckelworths aren't coming."

NINE

I GOT my courage up and was set to meet Raven after school Friday when a messenger from the principal's office came into my last-period class with a note in her hand. It was for me. It said:

> Ace Hobart,
> This is to report a math deficiency. Immediately after eighth period you are to report to Room 117 for remedial work and makeup.

At the bottom it said I hadn't handed in any homework and that I'd gotten 55 on the pop quiz Thursday morning and 35 on the one this morning. All this was true, but I never expected anything like this so soon. In Guttenberg it took weeks for bad news to filter back to students and parents.

Prior to calling your parents in for conference with the teacher and grade counselor, we are sending you this report. Failure to appear today

will deny you admittance to class Monday and
cause an immediate suspension until the conference is held.

They were sadists. They had me. I'd hate to see Dad
if somebody called him in to confer about me and my
math. He'd have to take off from work, lose a day's
pay . . . Besides, I couldn't let him come here—he'd
see my patch.

When the bell rang I found Raven waiting at the
door. "Hey, look, I'm sorry about this afternoon, but I
just got this mean letter from the principal. Look at it!"

She did and her face clouded over. "You got a 35.
Ace! What are you doing with all your time, man!
You gotta study . . . Wait a minute." She stopped chew-
ing me out and gave me the once over with her eyes.
"Listen, you worried about the Falcons?"

"What do you mea—"

"George gets straight A's. It's okay to be smart—
nobody said you have to be a dummy." She handed
the note back and started for the front door. I followed,
stunned by her reaction; I'd expected sympathy. She
pushed the door open and started down the sidewalk.
For a second I thought she wasn't going to say goodbye. But then she turned.

"Oh, rats! I'm sorry about this afternoon too. Bye!"
she whispered, blowing a kiss.

"Bye!" I whispered back, memorizing her expression.
I zoomed over to Room 117. It took me a whole hour
with Mr. Epstein's student teacher to settle down and
think about absolute values and the domain of the

variables. Afterward I thanked him; he had no idea he'd just ruined my love life.

Although Raven had said she and her family usually shopped late on Friday afternoons, I had to go over on the chance that she might be home. I even stopped in Gristede's for flowers. But when I rang the bell there was no answer. Then I noticed a note sticking out of the mailbox.

> Gone to the *mercado* with Mamacita and the kids but thank heavens there's tomorrow. Want to pick me up at nine so we can ride the bus to the shooting together? xxx Raven.

I tore off the bottom of the paper and wrote, "Yes, xxx Ace," wondering if I should write more x's than she did. But then I thought that would just call attention to it and so left it as it was. I put her note to me in the pocket close to my heart and went home carrying all the daisies I'd bought at Gristede's except one. I'd stuck that in the Galvez mailbox along with my reply.

It started to drizzle before I got home and it made the windows of the buildings I passed look streaked and sad. When I took off my patch at the apartment door, it was soggy.

Nora was in the living room with the radio turned up. She looked like she was trying to dance the frazzle, but as I came in she stopped. I had to do something with the flowers so I handed them to her.

"A bouquet! This blows my mind. What are you giving them to me for? Huh? Are you stoned?"

"They're for you is all," I said. That's when I got the idea. "Nora, how would you like to earn fifteen bucks?"

"How'd you know I need money? I got to get a hair dryer. Wait a minute! What do I have to do?" She wrinkled her nose suspiciously. "Horace! What do I have to do?"

"Can you keep a secret? You won't tell anybody?"

Her eyes narrowed. "Okay."

"You have to watch the reception desk at the Riviera Hotel tomorrow. You have to look grown up and hand out mail and keys."

"Would I meet a lot of people?"

"All kinds."

"Fifteen dollars?"

I nodded.

"For how long?"

"Oh, just a few hours. I'm not sure."

"Where will you be? Why don't you do it? How'd you get a job to give out?"

"None of your business. If you have to ask all these questions . . ." I started out of the room.

She zoomed after me. "Wait! Okay. But tell me what you're doing."

"Sometime. *If* you do the job right."

She looked at me hard, her eyes like X rays. "Horace, have you become a pusher?"

"Cut it out! I'm taking back the offer."

"Okay, okay, just had to check. When do I start?"

"Tomorrow. Be ready at nine sharp. And you'll have to keep quiet. Think you can figure out an alibi? You may need it."

"You mean for Mom?"

"Yeah."

"I could say Kelly Constantini wants me to play over at her house. Is that okay?"

"It's okay."

Early the next morning I sneaked into the bathroom before anybody was up to get ready for the shooting. A loose tile had popped up in the floor and I busted into it. "Oww!" I yelled.

When the throbbing stopped, I looked in the mirror. The sty was totally gone. But a pimple was near my ear—one of the sore kind. After working on it awhile, I showered, shampooed, and creme-rinsed. Then I pared my toenails. Didn't have to do anything to my fingernails; they were down to the quick already.

Every other second I'd be hit in the pit of my stomach with the realization that I was going to make a movie. I couldn't act! And grooming wasn't going to make me an actor. Still I kept working.

I remembered reading that Burt Reynolds shaves his armpits before shootings. If he didn't, he'd get sweat circles on his hand-tailored shirts when he does action scenes. So even though it seemed kind of fruity, I hauled out Mom's razor. Dad's would have scalped me. I raised my arm, put the razor to my skin and started coming down through the fuzz.

"Let me in! Let me in!"

Nora. I jerked and nearly slit my arm.

"Hey, Horace, what're you putting on? Smells like a perfume factory through the keyhole."

I dropped the razor fast; she'd tell. "Horace, I gotta *go*. Let me in. I want to get dressed for the job."

"Keep your mouth shut, hey!" I whispered, combing my hair above the patch.

She beat on the door. "Horace!" She made me screw up the part.

"Shut up!"

"Horace, kiddo." Dad's voice drilled through the door. He must have been right outside. "We're trying to get a little sleep this morning, your mother and I. Would you let your sister in there, please? If you can't share, you're welcome to use the facilities down the street at the public library."

"Gimme a break!" I whined. "Just wait another minute." I was finally getting the part right. I heard Dad stamp back down the hall.

Nora started to cry. "Can't wait. Owww!"

"Okay, okay, okay!" I ripped off the patch and let her in, messing up my hair. She shot past, crunching down on my hurt toe, hardly waiting for me to close the door after her. "Take it easy," I said on the other side.

"Kiddo!" Dad moaned from the bed. "Knock it off!"

When we were both finally ready, Nora and I left the apartment together. She locked the door with the key hanging on the chain around her neck.

"You must be going somewhere important to smell that good," she said.

"Maybe I'll tell you if you do the hotel job right. Then I'll know you can keep a secret."

We started down. After a few seconds Nora said, "Horace, can you wait a minute? Can we stop?"

We were on the third-floor landing, and when I

turned to her, she took my hands in her small warm ones and looked at me. "Horace, I promise I'll do whatever you say and I promise I can keep a secret."

For the first time in her life, she looked like a nice kid. Still—I didn't tell her. "Thanks, Nora, thanks. Now come on."

We hit the next landing and who should be coming up the stairs but Frieda Feckelworth and Calvin and Hilda. I was stunned. Nora and I turned and looked at each other.

Mrs. Feckelworth said, "Hello, Horace, Nora. We were able to come after all!"

"Surprised, old buddy?" Calvin said. He was wearing a shocking-pink T-shirt that said "This Is Your Life. It's Not a Dress Rehearsal."

"Oh—no—no—not at all! I should have expected it. Uh—how are you, Mrs. Feckelworth? Calvin? Hilda?"

"Fine! We're all fine! Cold's over!" the Feckelworths said, all talking together, looking happy and gazing all around the hall and stairways of our building.

Calvin suddenly smiled and said, *"Horatii curiosa felicitos?"* When I didn't answer, his face fell. "Forgotten your Latin already, Horace? You've only been here a week."

"Uh—ha ha—ha."

"It's from *The Satyricon,*" he said.

"Oh." I said. It didn't ring a bell.

"Tch-tch-tch," Calvin said in the same voice our Latin teacher had often used.

"I can't wait to see your mother. Is this the way up?" Mrs. Feckelworth said.

"Yes, sorry, there's no elevator."

"That's all right," she said too quickly. "Would you please show us the way?"

Nora gritted her teeth and turned around. "Horace has someplace important to go, so I'll take you up."

"Can I go with you, old buddy?" Calvin said.

Where'd he get the "old buddy"? In Guttenberg I was always trying to escape him.

"How about it?" he said.

"Calvy can't wait to renew an old friendship," said his mother.

Calvin blushed, making his face a little paler than his shirt.

Please don't let the Falcons see him, I prayed. I felt sick, but said, "Okay, if you want to. I guess he can take your place, Nora, now that you've got Hilda here—"

Nora was looking over the bannister at me, ready to burst into tears. "Yeah, Horace. Good luck and everything."

It made me feel sorry for her. I raised my hand and gave her an O with my thumb and forefinger as sort of a promise I'd make it up to her.

"Come on, Calvin we've got to beat it."

On the way I told him I'd taken this secret job working at the desk of a famous hotel in order to help the folks financially.

"Gee, I didn't think children could get jobs like that in New York City."

"Nobody here thinks I'm a child."

"Oh." He was quiet and seemed to be thinking. "I'm glad it's a famous one. Some hotels, you know, are just fronts for drug dealers. I read about one where there was a shoot-out and it ruined the revolving door."

"The door? Oh!"

Calvin looked at me suspiciously.

"Want to hear about the job?" I said quickly. "See, I come and let off Webber, who's there manning the desk now. But today—" I remembered my patch suddenly, pulled it out of my pocket, and slipped it on.

"What's that?" Calvin yelled.

"Just my patch."

"What's it for? I can't believe that!"

"Uh—the eye doctor said—I should wear it on bright days. I got eye strain. Too much light is bad for me." I checked the sky. There was sun.

"No kidding? Are you serious?"

"We're almost there. Let me tell you about the job."

"It makes you look really weird, know that? I don't think I'd wear it in pub— Hey! You don't wear it to school!"

"But today the reason I can't be at the desk is because I've got something special to do—I got to go to the eye doctor and a—"

"Son of a gun! I can't get over how you look."

"Get smart, Calvin—nobody mentions it."

"Oh."

"Nora was going to take over at the Riviera—this is even better. You'll get a kick out of sitting there for a little while. You like interesting people, don't you?"

"If they're smart, sure! It won't take too long, will it?"

"Oh, no!"

"And you'll still have time to show me around the Big Apple?"

"Sure, don't worry. Where do you want to go?"

When we got to the hotel Webber was straightening a pile of newspapers for sale on the desk. I saw him put the one he was reading when we came in under the bottom of the pile. I introduced Calvin to him. Webber didn't look as if he'd spent much time grooming himself, but he did have a different flowered tie on. It took him about two minutes to show Calvin the register, mailboxes, keys, and so on. Calvin stood behind the counter examining everything and grinning. "Looks okay," he said, reading the names on the register.

"Let's hurry, Webber, we're late already."

"Horace, why is Webber going to the eye doctor's with you?" Calvin said, looking up from the book.

"It's the eye, ear, nose, and throat guy. Webber here has a nose problem." Webber looked surprised.

"Oh." Calvin banged the little desk bell. "This is cool, Horace—rings in the key of C."

"Back *soon*," Webber said, winking at me and letting me step into the revolving door first.

"Hey! Is this the place where the drug pushers were shot down?" Calvin called. "Hey—hey!"

TEN

WEBBER AND I picked up Raven at her place and we walked to First Avenue together to take the bus uptown. She was wearing a gold lamé Windbreaker and she was so rosy cheeked I had to quit looking at her or I'd have gotten excited. I'd have had sweat stains for sure on my shirt. On the bus I held my arms out from my sides, being careful at the same time not to poke her or Webber beside me. When we were almost there she leaned over and gave me a big kiss. "I'm so thrilled, Ace!" Gimme a break, I thought. As Nevada would say, "Don't mix business and pleasure unless you can take the heat." Whew! Was I glad when we finally got off the bus.

One block over on Ninety-third was the location. A bunch of vans and Avis rental trucks were parked outside the park, which looked more like a bomb site. The concrete was humped up as though something had exploded underneath it and the sandbox was a pigsty. The movie crew was swarming over it with cameras and lights and lugging black rubber electric cords across the concrete. Everybody had on hats—all kinds, from baseball caps to sombreros.

When we walked through the gates, we saw Marilyn Maroon yelling at two guys in New York Yankee caps. They were unpacking a wooden crate marked PROP-ERTY. The minute she saw us, she stopped and rushed over. But the famous come-on smile was missing. "Where're the rest of the guys?" she demanded, her black eyes flashing at the three of us, giving us an instant once-over. She was wearing a white skirt and maroon silk shirt with rolled cuffs and she was all business.

"They'll be here, they'll be here," I said, remembering to hold my arms out from my sides again. That Marilyn was really built. I hadn't noticed before.

"I expect *talent* to get here on time. That was four minutes ago," she said, checking her big-faced watch glaring up with black numerals from her arm. Suddenly distracted, she started off toward François, who was seated at a card table. "Look around. See what you can learn," she said over her shoulder, "You, too, Raven." She hadn't looked at her except for the once-over.

Webber made a face and calmly unfolded a news-paper he'd bought at a newsstand and started to read. It was called *Showbiz*. Raven sat down on one of the crummy benches and pulled a big plastic mirror out of her shoulder bag. I wandered off alone to inspect things. I kept glancing back at the gate to see if the Falcons had come. *They couldn't let me down!* Over behind a bench a guy was down on his knees painting red blotches on the cement.

"If you don't mind, what's that for?" I asked.

The guy, in jeans, with a bare chest and eight million tattoos, said, "Your fence's blood, Mr. Hobart, kid." He grinned.

He knew me, Wow! "But don't you paint that after my fence is mugged and killed?" I asked.

"Not everything goes in sequence."

"Oh." I had a lot to learn. But he'd called me Mr. Hobart like I was somebody special. At home the folks treat me the same as Nora.

Still no sign of the Falcons. I started over to ask Raven what she thought had happened, when I heard some guys I couldn't see cursing and yelling. A blood-curdling scream from somewhere beyond the park raked my eardrum. I looked toward the street, but then I figured it was coming from behind the park, where there was a highway and the East River. I saw Raven stiffen and look around. Her eyes scanned the horizon. Could it be the Falcons? Suddenly I saw the four of them running through the gate. Freddy, in the lead, moved light and easy, but his eyes were dark. He was turning his head and looking behind them.

I ran over to him. "What's up? Did you hear that yelling?" His neck vein throbbed.

No answer. George and Slick, behind him, split to check out what was to the left and to the right in the park. Strolling in last was J.D. with the cuff on his left leg rolled high, doing his fancy walk, which seemed to scoop up the distance between us and make it disappear.

He grinned. "So what's up? They makin' the movie yet?" Little beads of sweat decorated his upper lip.

His shirttail was out, hanging below his jacket. George and Slick came back and joined us. I noticed Marilyn at the card table checking the Falcons over. J.D. quickly tucked his shirt in when he saw her.

"Marilyn's bugged you're late," I said in a low voice. "You still want to do it, don't you?" They looked on edge. Something was going on, but they weren't telling me.

Freddy shrugged. The rest of them were nervously watching the fence. "You're not worried, are you?" I said at last.

"About what?" Freddy said real fast in an irritated voice.

About your criminal abilities being exposed, is what I thought. But I said, "About your acting?"

"It's no worse than yours!" George snapped, and from then on looked at *me* as if I'd done something to him personally. Everybody, I noticed, though, looked mad at George.

"That's what I mean," I said. Nobody laughed.

Marilyn, who'd been in such a great rush before, didn't even look at us, much less call us. So we started roaming around the place. I showed the guys the blood spill and we watched the camera people set up. Webber was snoozing and Raven reading a Nevada Culhane book I'd lent her. She was half through it already. I noticed, even though there was a good wind coming off the river, that nobody's hair was blowing. There wasn't a person there who hadn't sprayed on something. Even tough gangs today know about grooming. TV does it. Everybody's *aware*. That's why people aren't embarrassed now to be on shows and say they're criminals or perverts, things like that. Anybody can get to be a star.

We must have hung around there for two hours, looking glum, mad, nervous, or bored, before Marilyn finally came over and said, "Time for makeup. Line up over there in front of that green van." It was outside the gate. "Webber, you too."

A man named Philby did our makeup. He wanted me to remove the patch, but when I said I couldn't, he seemed too embarrassed to insist. He had small hands and worked very gently on that side of my face. When I looked in the mirror afterward I saw he hadn't gotten any makeup on the patch.

We all came out looking not much different from when we went in. All except Webber. He was supposed to be my fence and they wanted him to resemble a famous racketeer. Webber said, "Philby hung up a picture of this guy wanted by the Post Office and tried to make me look like it." His upper teeth were blacked out and he had a mean mustache.

"Webber, it's not the Post Office who wants criminals," said Slick, spitting for emphasis. "It's the F.B.I."

Everybody looked amazed; Slick wasn't your smartest.

"Same thing," Webber said, wobbling off to the van marked COSTUME.

The Falcons and Raven and I were standing there when two cop cars came cruising down the street. They slowed and the police inside peered into the park. Then one pulled to the end of the block and stopped and the other backed up and stopped. Some officers got out and set up a wooden barricade halfway across the street. I checked the Falcons' expressions to see if they were thinking what I was: the cops were after them. But no! They looked *happy* to see the cops; I couldn't figure it out.

The police put up a sign on the road: MAYOR'S OFFICE FOR MOTION PICTURES, NYC. Their roadblock allowed only one lane of traffic at a time, where there were usually both east and west. In no time cars were honking and the street beyond us on either side jammed with cars. I saw one guy get out of a shiny black car and shake his fist. He looked exactly like Uncle Jake. I was set to wave when I noticed a woman with him. Lots of yellow bleached blond hair? That wasn't Aunt Betty. Couldn't be. Anyway, Jake was supposed to be in Chicago at a wholesale rice distributors' convention. Aunt Betty had called Mom from Hoboken last night and said he wasn't coming home till Sunday.

Funny, though, how in a big city like New York you're always seeing people who look like somebody you know.

"Hobart! Get in here!" a woman yelled from the door of the costume van, her voice like a whip. When I walked in she said, "I'm Rio, waddya got under da shirt?" She said *da shirt* like it rhymed with Detroit.

"Just my T-shirt."

"Take it off! Ya gotta leave your shirt unbuttoned for dis part. What are ya, dumb? Yer not some mama's goody-baby now. Not for dis! Yer a real nasty kid, you are. Ha! Ha!"

Ha ha! I thought back, wanting to pop her in the teeth. She pulled off my T-shirt without messing up my makeup, running her mouth the whole time. I was buttoning my shirt back up when she yelled, "Not all the way up! Leave it there!"

She undid the two top buttons again and opened the shirt, revealing my baby bald chest. She handed me the red jacket to put on. As soon as I got out the door I closed the buttons. I wasn't going to stand around that way.

Before I hit the ground she yelled, "Open them buttons!"

Over her I suddenly heard a whole bunch of voices yelling, "Open them buttons!" and then hee-hawing. What the . . . ? I looked over to one side and saw five of the tallest giants I'd ever seen sprawled against the iron fence posts. They looked as if they were either going to ooze through them, climb over them, or knock them down. They were shaking the bars like a jungle gym.

"*Who* are *they*?" I asked the Falcons, standing bunched in a knot by the costume van.

J.D. whispered, "Piranhas."

"Looka that!" Freddy said, clenching his fists. "Never expected to see a Monsoon talkin' to a Piranha."

Next to the Piranhas stood four mean-looking no-neck guys in black shirts and pants, their faces blank. Monsoons. While the Piranhas were moving all over, the Monsoons were still as rocks.

"What time it is?" Raven muttered. "I'm getting sick of hanging around here."

"We've been here a little over two hours—it takes forever to make movies," Freddy said.

"How do you know?" George said, sounding half mad.

Freddy opened his hands and raised them. "My brother told me. He was an extra once. Said the waitin' drove him crazy. But I got the patience to do anything long as it's important." He went on, "When you're born in a cave like I was in the D.R. you get to be that way, y'know? Patient. Maybe I'll be the first caveman that's made a success in the movies. See, I'm gonna be famous."

When he was finished, no one said anything. Freddy didn't talk much, so I was proud and I guess the others were, too, that he'd tell us that about himself. I was wishing I knew something about George and Slick and J.D. too.

"Looka that! Looka that!" Slick said. "Now there's Wart-Hogs here too." Three more tough-looking guys —in striped T-shirts. "That's the gang that replaced the Unquenchable Fires when they went to Sing Sing."

They were all looking at *us*. For the first time since I joined the Falcons I felt scared. Gangs! New York was swarming with them! Wart-Hogs! Monsoons! Piranhas! No use worrying about sweat stains now. My whole shirt was turning into one. "What are they here for?" I said. "How'd they know we were filming?"

"*Somebody*," Freddy said slowly, "told 'em."

Everybody said, "Not me, not me!" except George. He said, "Maybe they saw it in the *Daily News*?"

"Bull! You were bragging about it to Stab Evans

and some of the other Piranhas in the army-navy store
yesterday!" J.D. hollered. The guys at the fence started
to cackle and make other mocking noises. J.D. looked
at me suddenly. "I'm not scared of them, are you?"

"Uh—ha ha ha—*no*!"

A film crew guy came running over to hand us sandwiches out of a big white box marked ORNSTEIN'S—
Bound and Gagged lunch. I looked at the fence and
saw four Wart-Hogs now, five Piranhas, who looked
as if they'd been stretched on poles, and four Monsoons
—thirteen vicious guys. I was almost wishing I was
back in the apartment playing Risk with Calvin.

ELEVEN

AT TWO we started the mugging scene. Marilyn had told us that Webber and I were partners in crime. I was a robber; Webber, the fence. The Falcons (known as Night's Messengers in the movie) were mad at me for ripping off a store in their neighborhood. So in the scene they were chasing me to recover what I'd stolen.

"You're waiting in the park, Ace, for Webber to come," Marilyn said, leaning over the bench where she'd told me to sit. "He's going to take the goods—seven watches—off you and find a buyer."

Then she told the Falcons where to stand and how to move across the park toward me on the bench. We blocked the scene's movements exactly eleven times. Then the camera moved forward and the shooting began.

Raven put down the mystery she'd finished. "What am I supposed to do?" she asked.

Marilyn didn't answer. A technician wearing a Sherlock Holmes cap brought his light and turned it on.

"Make it nighttime," Marilyn said.

"Got it!" the cameraman answered.

I looked at Freddy. He shrugged. "Filters, man, nuttin' to it. They can make day night or night day. They just stick 'em on the lens."

"Ready, Messengers! Stoop low—you're on the prowl. Freddy, pay attention!" Marilyn yelled.

There was a hiss from the iron fence. I looked over and saw the guys from the gangs laughing. The Falcons stooped low, Slick getting the lowest of all, his butt high in the air. They crossed over the walk from the gate to a point about ten feet from where I was on a bench, waiting for Webber. Marilyn made them do it again.

The technical guys brought lamps over and adjusted them near the Falcons. They did the same movements again and again while the crew moved the equipment, made adjustments, and talked among themselves.

As the minutes passed, the Piranhas, Monsoons, and Wart-Hogs, who were watching in the evil way cats watch little birds, were getting louder. Nobody seemed to mind, but it gave me the goose bumps. Suddenly Slick winced and jolted up straight and grabbed a spot on his rear. He quickly took his hand away and checked to see if Marilyn had noticed him. Then he glared bullets at the kibitzers at the fence, who by this time were hooting and hollering.

"Night Messengers! Get together and plan the mugging. Ace, cover your ears! This is supposed to be natural, so you can't listen." Marilyn looked at me hard. "Tighter! Clamp those ears!"

I clamped, but still tried to hear. No way! I had to guess what they were going to do to me.

While the Falcons huddled and were filmed, I sat

sweating in the hot sunshine, ears covered, trying to figure what they'd come up with. If I wasn't tough back, they'd discover me, Ace the fake! Raven, at the side, shot mad looks at me and began to pace up and down. I'd hoped Marilyn would let her mug, too, but when it came up, Marilyn said no.

Freddy yelled something and Marilyn signaled them to go ahead. I uncovered my ears and heard a putt-*ting* on the metal strut of the bench where I was sitting. Those bird haters were trying to get me!

I acted like nothing happened.

"Ready, Mrs. Maroon," Freddy yelled.

"Call me Marilyn. Okay, now I want you to get this scene cinema verité style for realism, so you mug Ace, and, Ace, you resist as you naturally would."

"Glorifying violence," Raven muttered.

"Try not to hurt each other too much, but be serious." Marilyn then looked over her shoulder at Raven. "Violence is where the money is. Don't like it any more than you do." She looked at the cameraman. "Ready?"

"Ready!" he said, and my heart started to thump like it wanted out of my chest. This was *it!*

Someone came up with the take number on a board and snapped it in front of the camera.

"Roll em!" shouted Marilyn, and the filming began.

I checked my shirt pocket for the seven watches Property had given me and tried to concentrate on counting them and looking out for Webber. I tried not to think of the Falcons sneaking up.

Something cold pressed against my neck. "Don't make a move!" J.D. muttered.

George and Slick came around the front of the bench and loomed over me. Slick spit. George said, "Hand over everything ya got or we'll cut ya!" His eyes were mean. Freddy at one side was the lookout.

"I can't reach for anything, man—that guy there told me not to make a move." Meaning J.D.

George and Slick frowned. "Hand over them watches!" said Slick.

"Get outta here!" I said in my foghorn.

The Falcons looked surprised. Freddy said, "Come on, you guys!" in a desperate tone, his face dark and scary-looking. He was into this. Putt-*ting* went something against my bench again.

"So whata we do now?" Slick said. I couldn't tell if he was talking to me or Freddy. It seemed he wanted someone to give him directions. Maybe Marilyn. I heard some smart-ass tittering from the sides and then Slick winced and jolted up again; his face turned furious. I don't know what those guys were flipping over here but they must've stung poor Slick again. The camera was bearing down on his face and he cursed.

"Get the loot, man!" J.D. yelled. "Go *on*!"

George looked mortified and poked his finger at my chest. "Gimme the stuff—come—" He wasn't even pushing.

I didn't move because I thought they should scare me more. Slick was staring at me, then at the camera, and not doing a thing.

"Slick, get with it! He's wide open!" J.D. yelled.

"What d'ya want me to do? You're standin' in the wrong place for me to wrassle him."

A hoot went up from the fences.

"What d'ya mean? This is where I *said* I'd be!"
J.D.'s face busted out in sweat all over. My own sweat
was dripping down my neck.

"Cu-u-u-t!" Marilyn yelled. "What's going on here?
You're just standing around gassing! That's not mugging."

All the guys spoke at once. "J.D.'s in the wrong
place!"

"So Slick's not doing his part!"

"Ace ain't scared and won't cooperate."

"Freddy was supposed to say, 'Gimme your stuff,'
too!"

They were furious and yelling at each other. I had
never seen them like that before.

Marilyn said, "Well, is this the way you usually do
it?"

I was sure they'd say, "We're not telling all our
secrets," but they just looked at each other, sheepish,
embarrassed, shifting their feet back and forth and
shrugging their shoulders. They didn't look like my
Falcons anymore. I wanted to help them.

"Well, you *know* how to mug, don't you?" Marilyn
said.

Freddy cleared his throat. "How about we try it
again, men?"

He was so proud, I think it was hard for him to say
that, and I was glad he didn't give up. They went
back in front of the cameras and tried again. This time
they didn't roll the film.

Marilyn, whose eye makeup had started to run in
the heat, looked at François and said, loud enough for

anyone to hear, "So much for cinema verité. I have to teach the muggers how to mug."

There was a hoot, cackling, and loud whistling from the sidelines and I looked up. The Piranhas were waving their long arms and laughing and pointing at us. The Wart-Hogs in their striped shirts were too. But not the Monsoons—they were still just silently staring as if they were watching a freak show.

"Put us in the movie, come on! *We'll* make it exciting," one tall guy yelled. "You can get a real thriller out of the Piranhas—ssss!"

Raven suddenly jumped off the bench and raised her fists in the air, then slowly, like a stalking panther, she circled us, staring at each of us in a fierce, clenched-jaw way. I stared back a moment, mesmerized, and felt an incredible power coming from her as if her concentration was giving us guts. Then I remembered! *Incredible Power*—that was the Nevada Culhane book she'd been reading, and Nevada himself had used the very same trick to inspire the victims in that book to fight back against their evil captors. She was giving us her power! She wasn't going to let us be mocked.

This time, film running, we *did it*. J.D. throttled me with a hammerlock around the neck. I grabbed his fists and tried to twist them off me. Slick and George pulled me clear off the bench and held my legs in the air. Freddy, seeing I was powerless and voiceless even, just whisked the watches out of my pocket. Then they dumped me on the bench and took off out of camera range. I fell back clutching my sore throat.

"Excellent!" cheered Marilyn, and François beamed.

I was so hot and elated when the scene was finished, I had to take off my jacket to cool down. Raven, with an ironic smile, came over and said, "I see you gave her what she wanted."

"Thanks for your help," I said.

"I didn't do anything."

I gave her a special look, letting her know I knew she had. She blushed and looked away.

The gangs wrapped around the fences started to chant. I couldn't make out the words, but it was unnerving. "You know these guys?" I said.

She nodded. "You kidding? Not personally. Toughest guys in the city."

"Oh? I thought the Falcons were."

She smirked. "Come *on*, Ace! The Wart-Hogs are from Brooklyn, the Monsoons from the South Bronx, and the Piranhas terrorize Canal Street."

"Hey, baby! Tell 'em to put us in the show!" One of the Piranhas yelled. He was dancing around with his arms swaying wildly, so tall it looked as if he could have walked over the fence.

Raven spun around and glared at him. "Who are you calling baby, you #30!8XF2?!!*$!*?"

I never heard such filth in all my life! The voice didn't even sound like Raven's! It was as rough as anything I'd ever heard in the city. I'm not kidding. The guy blanched. Raven screamed, "Dirty chauvinist!" The cops by the barricades heard her, went up, and chased the gangs away.

"That's it for now," Marilyn said after they'd finished filming the next sequence with Webber lying on the ground in the pool of his painted blood. "François has the cards with your location tonight. It's the water-front scene. Pier 42 off Morton Street. Be there at eight sharp! Any questions? No? Go see him and pick them up right away."

The crew started to move out. Freddy said, "Let's just hang around, waddya say? J.D., Slick! Pick up the cards from Franshaw—hurry up."

"I'll get 'em," Slick said.

"Give those rotten Wart-Hogs and the other animals a chance to get far away first, right? Huh, Freddy?" J.D. asked.

"Sure!" George said.

"Don't wanna rub their noses in our fame, right, George?"

"Right! Those guys are just jealous."

Webber was nudging my side. "Want to ask Marilyn to give us our money so we can pay off Calvin Feckel-worth? Heh! Maybe, we can get them to pay him—you know. Business expenses, huh?"

François overheard him. "You don't get paid till we're done like the contract said."

"Darn!"

"Don't forget your jacket, Ace!" Raven said as we walked to the gate.

"Oh, yeah!" I ran back to the bench where I'd dropped it but it wasn't there. "Hey, Marilyn! Seen my jacket?"

She was helping François fold up the card table. "No, and I've got to run."

I ran to the costume van, but it was locked and Rio wasn't around. Half the crew had left already.

"It isn't here! Where's my jacket?" I shouted. "Hey!

Anybody seen my red jacket with the dragon on it?"

George, J.D., Slick, and Freddy came and helped me look, Webber had gone on ahead. But it was no good. The jacket was gone.

Suddenly we stopped still in the middle of the park. We looked at each other. Then George said slowly, "Bet I know who took it."

I felt sick.

George and Freddy said, at the same time, "The Piranhas."

J.D. said, "Or the Monsoons. They're real bad. But the Wart-Hogs are worse." Then he looked around the fringes of the park very slowly. There weren't any gang members I could see from where we stood in the park, but we moved out of there in one body, Freddy at the front with George, then Raven and me with Slick on the other side of her, and J.D. bringing up the rear.

It was one of the spookiest times in my life. We left the location and went up Ninety-third to Second for a bus. For some reason the sidewalks on both sides were empty of people and all the doorways seemed suspicious.

Just as we passed a candy store, someone lunged out at us and yelled, "Boo!"

We stopped so short that Raven and Freddy bumped heads and J.D.'s boot came crunching down on my foot like a hammer, hitting the toe I'd blasted in the morning.

"Owww!" everybody screamed. "Webber! What the devil—"

"It was a joke! I was just getting you all candy bars. What are you, scaredy cats? I'm just a little old guy." He waved a handful of chocolate bars in front of us. "Here."

Everybody took one. "Thanks," I said, "but I can't eat right now, I just lost my jacket—"

"Somebody stole it!" George said. "The dumb guy leaves his stuff all over." I turned and looked at George; I'd never seen him so ticked off.

"Why're you taking it out on him?" asked Freddy.

"*I* ain't got it," Webber said, unwrapping a peanut Venus bar. "What're you going to do, Ace?"

"I don't know," I said, trying to figure George out.

Everybody stood on the corner, waiting for the downtown bus and eating candy until it came. We were going to change at Twenty-third for the crosstown bus. I was looking for a seat next to Raven, but she squeezed in between George and Freddy, so I sat on the end of the row of Falcons. Webber plopped down next to me. I guessed Raven didn't like me without my jacket. Maybe she sees me now for what I am. Don't cry, Ace, I thought gloomily, you still have the fun of seeing Calvin at the end of this ride. Boy, was I bushed! I leaned my head back against the window and closed my eyes, longing for a piece of oblivion.

"Don't shut your eyes, man! We gotta look sharp for the Piranhas and company," Freddy yelled down the line. I sat up and stared out the window.

TWELVE

THE FALCONS and Raven got off the crosstown bus a couple stops before it pulled to the curb in front of the Riviera. We walked in through the door. My heart sank. Calvin was sitting on the stool, arms hanging at his sides, eyes closed.

"Webber, look!" Maybe the pushers got him, I thought in one insane moment of alarm.

Webber burst out laughing. "He's asleep, Ace! Just asleep. I done it myself a dozen times. This place can put anybody under." He wiped his eyes.

I stared at Calvin until he moved. He wrinkled his face, opened his eyes, and when it registered who it was looking at him, his pale face turned purple. "There you are!" he snarled.

"Calvin—"

"Can't tell me you've been at an eye doctor's for *hours*! Horace Hobart, wait until I tell your mother what you did to me. I've been sitting here all day handing out mail and keys to drunks, dopes, and other dips. You promised to show me New York. You prom-

ised it would be only a little while until you came
back. I could have been reading *The Satyricon!* I could
have seen the Guggenheim, the map collection at the
Historical Society. Now it's too late! In fact, I don't
want to see it now. I wouldn't spend five minutes more
in this rotten cit—"

Suddenly he shut up. He looked behind me at something and I, imagining Piranhas, Wart-Hogs, and Monsoons, spun around so fast I nearly floored a very short
woman who was rushing up to me. "Hey!" I said.

"Hey!" she said back. "You're Ace Hobart, aren't
you? I want to talk to you. Bibi Plosser, NBS."

Calvin said, "Oh, brotherrr! Now what's going on
here? I can't take any more. Give me my money. Let
me just get out of here. I'm going back to Guttenberg.
My mother is *always* forcing you on me. I didn't want
to come in the first place. Forget New York! Blow up
the bridges, the Lincoln Tun—"

When he said what he'd said about his mother I
suddenly felt different toward him. I knew how he
felt! He grabbed the bills I was peeling off and I
handed him another. "For good measure," I said.

"*Tempus fugit,*" he said, spun around, and headed
for the door.

"*Tempus fugit,*" I said after him. "Thanks!"

"Yeah," Webber said. "Thanks a lot, kid."

Calvin muttered something under his breath as he
got into the revolving door. It sounded Latin but I
don't think they teach it in school.

"Well, Mr. Hobart?" the little woman who'd come
up and surprised us said. She looked like an executive

mouse in a gray business suit, rummaging inside her leather bag. "Here's my card. As I said, I'm Bibi Plosser from the *This Morning* show. Executive producer." She pointed at the card. "NBS."

My mouth dropped open.

"Sit down. I want to talk to you. I want to set up an interview with you for the *This Morning* show— okay, Ace? Dean Willit is interested in movies and teenagers and *he* wants to interview you on the show."

I don't *want* to be interviewed! I almost shouted.

"You know the show?" she asked.

"My folks watch it." They never missed it in fact.

"Wonderful—then you'll feel right at home."

"Oh, no—I can't be on thàt show! No way!"

"It's important to your movie. It'll make *Bound and Gagged* a success at the box office. Ask Marilyn."

"No."

"You're just shy—look at you!"

"Hey, really Ms. Plosser, I can't do that."

"But you'd be wonderful—just be yourself."

I began backing away from her.

"Ace, you're a very amusing young man," she said, coming toward me. "This will make you famous."

I shook my head.

"Mr. Hobart, it's not right for actors to keep themselves from their public," she said.

"Wait a minute. I don't have a public—ha ha—" I was getting close to the door.

"But you *will* have a public. Soon. Marilyn's already set it up."

I felt the revolving door behind me. "Bye, Webber!"

I called and, "Bye, Ms. Plosser, too!" I zoomed through and the sweet air of New York City hit my face.

When I got home I discovered I already had a public. My mom's voice was the loudest.

"Where have you been, Horace Hobart, and what did you do to Calvin Feckelworth? He came back when I was ready to serve dinner and threatened to kill his mother if they didn't go back to Guttenberg right away and here I am with a pot of chili and corn-bread all ready and Calvin said you didn't take him *anywhere*—that you pulled a trick on him and—" She stopped to take a breath.

So Pop filled in. "Hey, kiddo, what's the deal? Do you want to explain now or what?"

Nora's voice skidded above his. "Hilda is worse than ever, Horace. I'm sick! Why didn't you come back earlier? You're a rat! I'm not going to be your friend again. Ever!"

"I don't know how you could treat our friends that way, Horace," Mom said. "What's come over you? You're not the boy we brought from Guttenberg. Is he, Barney? He's different. Something's changed him." Suddenly Mom turned her attention to Dad and seemed mad at him. "Maybe *this* was a *mistake*—moving here—a big, *fat*—"

"Now, wait a minute! Lay off him, will ya?" Dad put up his hand. "Everybody ease off! It's not easy moving to a new town—especially one like New York City. It takes some doing, doesn't it, son?" I blinked, Dad had never called me "son" like *that* before. Usually it was Mom defending me. Dad put his arm gently around my shoulder. "He's got to get used to new people and new ways, don't you, Horace? So do I. So do you, honey," he said, suddenly including Mom in the hug. It didn't take Nora but a second to squeeze in between Dad and me.

"Me too," she said.

For a minute there was quiet. The only sound was the chili bubbling on the stove. I took a deep breath. Dad gave Mom a loud kiss.

"Hey! Who's for seeing the Rockettes at Radio City?" Dad said. "We could go tonight—"

"Oh, I'd like to, Pop," I said quickly, "but there's a get-acquainted party for new students at the Kennedy gym—remember, Mom! I told you yesterday."

She looked at me, her eyes a bit tired and dazed, and slowly nodded. "That's right. But can we afford the movies?" she said to Dad.

"We have to afford it! If the Hobarts are going to live in New York, they have to take advantage of the culture—right, Horace?"

"Right, Dad."

"That's my boy!"

THIRTEEN

IT WASN'T completely dark when I left The Pits after supper, but I got an anxiety attack realizing I didn't know how to get to the waterfront. I hadn't thought to ask anyone for directions that afternoon. The Falcons and I agreed to meet on location, so I was on my own. No jacket. No Raven (Marilyn had excluded her from the night sequences). Not even Webber. Just me, myself, and I trying to find Pier 42 off Morton Street. Which way was it?

"Ya gotta go down to Houston Street—then ya gotta go crosstown. Then ya gotta walk over a few blocks and . . ." a drunk with mahogany-colored teeth told me on Second Avenue. The whole time he was talking I was watching the foam collecting in the corners of his mouth and he was grinning at my eyepatch. Afterward he gave me a big slap on the back. "Get 'em good, Pirate!" he called after me.

To my surprise, he was reliable. Twenty minutes and two bus rides later I was walking along the eeriest, dirtiest, most deserted streets I'd ever seen. I mean *creepy*! One dilapidated warehouse after another. No people. Just things too dark and shapeless to identify—all of them looking like they were going to slither out of the shadows to strangle me.

I hurried from one dim streetlight to the next. Broken glass crunched under my feet. Other than that, it was absolutely quiet—the kind of quiet Dad says is in telephone repair centers, places where it's so sound-proof you can hear your own blood racing through your veins. Walking along Leroy Street, my blood sounded like Niagara. I carefully picked my way around warehouse entrances and battered garbage cans. Mostly the garbage cans. Nobody around there puts trash in them. Warehouse trash is too big. Worn-out truck tires, molding gunk, rotting floorboards—it's all strewn on the sidewalks and gutters like booby traps.

I kept heading west toward the river like the drunk told me. I thought if I pretended I was Nevada Cul-hane and hummed a few bars of "All the Little Fishies Gotta Swim," I'd feel better. I didn't. My humming only got on my nerves.

At the end of Leroy I came to West Street. I looked across and swallowed hard. To get to the other side where the piers were I had to walk *under* the West Side Highway, which was elevated. It was also being torn down. No traffic. No lights. No anything. From underneath all I could see were big black shadows stretching like canopies from one arched metal beam to another. It was a bad place to have a good imagina-tion. Starting across the cobblestones, my heart was throbbing and my rubber-soled sneakers sounded like horse hooves. Then I realized I wasn't alone.

Somebody else's feet were making the noise!

"Hey-yyyyy, man—that you?" The voice echoed through the steel beams, making me practically jump out of my skin when I heard it. "Hey-yyy—waitttt!"

I ducked behind the closest beam and peeked out. "Oh, ha ha. It's *you*, J.D."

"Yeah, heh-heh—it's you, man. I wasn't sure."

We walked the rest of the way under the highway together, then up past a pier with a huge, ugly warehouse. On the other side we were overjoyed to see the rental trucks and the crew setting up lights. Everything else along the waterfront was black, so Pier 42 looked like a carnival. George, Slick, and Freddy had gotten there ahead of us, and Philby was working on their makeup—heavy rings of black eyeliner around their eyes. "To emphasize the whites of their eyeballs," Philby explained. I thought they looked like ancient Egyptian thugs.

"You and J.D. want to hurry and get yours on, Horasis?" Marilyn called. "We're just about ready with the cameras."

J.D. got the eyeball treatment, but Philby greased my face with a mixture of clown white and mint green. Not heavy—just a thin coat—but enough to give my skin a transparent glow. Coming out of the makeup van, I looked up at the moon. It wasn't full; only a small sliver that had risen over the Hudson River, shedding about as much light on the waterfront as a baby lightning bug.

"Don't look much bigger'n a toenail clipping up there, does it, Ace?" Freddy said when he saw me looking at it.

"Right," I answered, struck by the sharpness of his observation.

Everything was ready to go. About fifty feet or so of camera tracks had been laid diagonally across the pier. Michael, the cameraman with the fixation on his Yankee cap, was sitting up in his tower seat, being coasted back and forth over the tracks. "Don't roll me into the water," he said to a couple of technicians.

There was a lot of joking going on with the crew, but none, I noticed, among the four cops patrolling the clearing between the pier and the dark labyrinth under the highway.

"Come, Horasis," Marilyn called. "Your director wants to direct you." She was in a much better mood than she had been this afternoon.

I followed her onto the pier and we picked our way through the maze of equipment that had been hauled down from the park only a couple of hours ago. Two scenes in one day—five hundred dollars. On a per diem basis, I was making almost as much as the President of the United States.

Marilyn stopped and did a quick estimate of our distance from the camera tracks, then marked a small x with chalk next to a grease spill. "This is where I want you to stop running, Horasis. When you get here, *freeze*. Look behind you. Shift your eyes. You're panicked and you're trying to see if anyone's chasing you from the warehouse. That's when the camera moves in for a close-up. On cue, turn your head toward the water. When you see what's coming up after you, your face has got to be a mask of terror—okay?"

Her hands went to her hips and she looked at François kneeling at the far end of the pier. "Hey, Sweetheart, how're things going?" she called to him. "You about ready?"

What, I wondered, was going to be coming up after me?

Taking my arm, she said, "He can't hear—the crew's making too much noise."

At first I thought François was alone, staring into the murky depths of the Hudson. When Marilyn and I got down there, I knew something kinky was going on . . . voices were coming from under the end of the pier. "Hey, man . . . what's that creakin' noise?" somebody was asking. "The *ropes, estúpido*," somebody answered. "The *ropes!*"

Sounded like Slick and Freddy.

I bent down between Marilyn and François, looking over the edge. All four Falcons were dangling over the water on a long, narrow scaffold that was swinging from some creaky ropes. I'd never seen anybody cling to ropes like they were. "See Slick's face?" Marilyn whispered to me. "That's the same expression I want you to have during the close-up."

"Sort of paralyzed?" I asked.

"Exactly." She yoo-hooed, trying to get their attention. "Hey, fellas—let's rehearse climbing up here. The cameras are ready to roll. We're wasting time."

There was no movement from below. A breeze

rocked the scaffold and I heard Slick whimper. "Shut up!" Freddy said. "You ain't the only one who can't swim."

"*Now!*" called Marilyn.

"Hear that? There it is again!" J.D. said. "The *noise!* It ain't ropes, man. Somebody's down here."

The other Falcons let out a cry. Then, without the aid of a ladder, all four of them sprang to the top of the pier. Slick was in the lead, his face so white he could've taken my part without greasepaint.

Marilyn was thrilled. "Bee-utiful," she crooned. "Every kid in America's going to scream himself *sick* watching this scene. It'll be a classic." She took my arm and began leading me back to the chalk mark. "Run the fellas through it one more time," she called to François. "With chains this time, and knives in their mouths."

I was sure glad I wasn't in their shoes. Nothing short of saving Raven's life could get me down on that scaffold if somebody was lurking around under the pier. Was there? Or was J.D. kidding? He sure sounded sincere.

"All right, Horasis," Marilyn said to me, "stand where you are, slightly crouched. That's it. Hey, Michael, show him where you'll be for the close-up." Two cameraman rolled Michael toward me on the tracks and Marilyn stood behind them, waving a small flag. "Whoa—stop. Right there. Can you see me, Horasis? I'm going to hold this up and when you see me drop it, turn, looking back at the end of the pier." Her arm dropped with the flag and I turned. François was arguing with the Falcons. It looked like they were balking about going down on the scaffold again.

François flailed his arms. The crew went dead quiet, watching, then we all listened. "All right," François shouted, dipping into his pocket, "ten *now*—and the other ten when you climb up again, okay?"

I really admired the Falcons when I saw them disappear over the edge.

At last we were ready. I don't know whether it was because we were tired, scared, or finally getting the hang of the movie business, but the whole scene couldn't have gone smoother if we'd rehearsed for a year. I didn't need flags or chalk marks. With everybody swallowed up in the darkness behind the cameras and lights, I really felt abandoned—terrified. A hush had fallen over the waterfront as well as the set, and all I could hear was the slap, slap of the river. I was so psyched up during my lonely run across the pier, it didn't occur to me nobody was really after me. I just automatically turned—right where I was supposed to—letting the cameras zoom in for the close-up.

The paralysis was no act. What I saw coming up over the end of the pier would have made anybody's face numb. *Four crazed killers!* I mean it. They weren't the Falcons anymore. Not with the kind of evil glint they had in their eyes. They were going to rip me apart with their knives.

I froze just as Marilyn wanted. My legs turned to stone, my feet anchors on the rotting wooden plank. My eyes rolled wildly inside my numb head and my jaw fell slack. I couldn't move. I wanted to scream, but my vocal cords were dead. My foghorn was gone. All I got out was something between a gag and a gargle—"*Aaraggghhhackkkk.*"

"Cu-u-u-tt," yelled Marilyn, then she and the crew clapped.

That was it. One shooting had done it. There wasn't any need for retakes. Later, when we gathered for coffee outside the makeup van, Marilyn gushed over me, telling me my performance was "the ultimate portrait of terror." Everybody on the set nodded like they agreed. Even the Falcons.

"Yeah, ya shoulda seen your face, Ace," Slick said. "You woulda thought we was gonna chop you up in little biddy hunks or something."

Then George wanted to know how I'd made that sound down in my throat.

"It's his natural talent," Marilyn answered for me. "He has the potential for becoming a brilliant, *brilliant* actor."

There were a lot of hoots and whistles when she leaned over to give me a big, juicy kiss. I remember I didn't know what to do with my hands. Let them hang? Put them behind my back? Finally I just shoved them into my jeans pockets. If anyone reported the incident to Raven, I didn't want her to think I'd been a willing party or anything. "You sex pistol," Marilyn whispered as she unclamped her lips from my cheek. "You're going to leave a new generation of women limp with desire."

I saw François watching both of us over the top of his plastic cup. "Oh, ha ha—that's a funny line, Mrs. Maroon," I said, acting like she'd told me a joke.

"It's no line," she said, wiping her maroon lipstick off my pale green face. "I happen to know what women like."

The Falcons were unusually quiet while we were in Philby's van cleaning off our makeup. Even Freddy seemed jumpy, and I noticed he cleared his throat each time he dipped his fingers into his jar of Pond's.

"You really think somebody was under the pier?" I asked J.D.

"You better believe it, man," he said, wiping around his eyes with a wad of tissues. "This place is crawlin' with Piranhas. They're out there waitin' for us."

Goose bumps the size of popcorn balls rose up and down my arms and the back of my neck. "How do you know?"

"The calls, man. Them were Piranha calls under the pier and over by the warehouse." J.D. cupped one hand around the other and blew between his thumbs making a noise something like a shrill coo. "Didn't you hear 'em doing that this afternoon?"

"I thought it was pigeons."

"*Pigeons?*" He thought I was kidding. "Man, don't anything ever corrupt your cool?" he said, breaking out in a big, nervous grin.

I glanced up at my face in the mirror we were sharing and wiped off a layer of makeup around my eyepatch. Underneath the makeup my clean skin had as much color as a bowl of whipped cream.

When we were leaving the van, ready to go home, everybody came up with the same idea at the same time: bumming a ride uptown with the Maroons.

"Betcha they beat it fast to skip paying us our extra

twenty for tonight," George grumbled when we saw their car was gone.

We'd started walking slowly toward the highway and everybody was irritable. "Ah, shut up," Freddy told George. "You was the one takin' longer'n anybody gettin' off your eyeliner."

"Yeah," added Slick. "Besides, you got two tens for sittin' over the water, didn't ya?"

That got to George, who was already in a nasty mood, and he started calling Slick "Chicken-Slicken." Then Slick got all huffy and asked George if he wanted to make something of it.

"Yeah, I'll make something of it," George hissed. "Next time you go blubbering like a chicken-licken jackass, I'll shove ya into the drink myself!"

I mean here we were with Piranhas all over the place, looking for us, and the Falcons were ready to start swinging. Why couldn't they get along like other groups? No one ever hears of 4-H members picking on each other.

"*Hey, fellas . . .*" somebody called.

We looked back at the pier. By now everybody had left except the camera crew. Michael and his men were packing up their equipment to load it onto the back of their van. "Don't take off yet," he hollered, waving his Yankee hat at us. "François left you some envelopes. Looks like play money for the weekend."

George swore and kicked his boot into some loose gravel. "Jerk! He stupid or something?"

"Man, I can't figure you," J.D. said. "One minute you're havin' a big spaz 'cuz you *didn't* get the money. And now—"

"*Shhhhh!*" George's eyes were scanning the darkness like radar antennae. "The Piranhas got a scout under the highway," he whispered.

"Holy sheez—the money! Now *they* know!" said J.D. "Man, they'd rub out their own mothers for less 'n a nickel."

George looked at him with disgust, then turned and asked Freddy if we should risk picking up the envelopes.

Freddy rounded his shoulders. "Waddya think, Ace?"

"You think a newcomer ought to make decisions?" I asked.

"This ain't the army."

"Well, I dunno," I said finally. "I don't need the money. What about the rest of you? You need it?"

I heard three "not me's," then Slick said, "Me neither," wiping his nose with the back of his hand. "Waddya say we beat it, guys?" he asked. "Hop a cab. We need to, we can even pay for it."

We all looked east toward the empty black streets stretching out from West Street under the elevated highway. Nothing. Not even a truck from a meat-packing house.

"Ya idiot. Where do you think we are—Times Square?" George snarled at Slick. "Cabbies don't cruise the waterfront!"

"*Hey, fellas—you gonna get these pay envelopes or not?*"

I turned to yell back to Michael that we'd decided to skip them, but he was already running after us with a flashlight.

"Listen," he said when he caught up, "I don't care if you don't want your money, but Marilyn said she'd have my head if I forgot to give you the instructions for the TV show."

"What TV show?" Freddy asked, looking at me. "What's he talkin' about?"

"Well—it's kind of a surprise," I said.

Not for long. Marilyn, the master organizer, had clipped five cards with the studio's address and the time we were to show up Monday onto the envelopes Michael was passing out. "Crap, would you believe this?" George said as he read his card with Michael's light. "She wants us there at six A.M." Then he swore and ripped open his attached envelope to see if his money was inside.

Each of us had a twenty with an individual note telling us if we acted natural and wore our regular street clothes we could do millions of dollars' worth of PR for the movie. "This is your chance to steal all your viewers' hearts," my note said at the bottom. "You'll see—a few days from now the name Horasis will be a household word. M.M. P.S. Try and round up another dragon jacket, okay?"

Oh, yeah, sure, I thought. Every other person has an uncle with bad taste who used to be a merchant marine. I was resigned to showing up at the studio in a T-shirt, then Freddy promised he'd dig up his brother Gregory's old gang jacket for me to wear. "Ain't bad," he said. "Green satin with the word *Marabunta* on it. Then the back's gotta giant ant. Y'know—the ones that eat people."

"Fine," I said. "Bring it."

A quarter to eleven. All of us were hedging. Nobody in his right mind would go down those creepy streets at that hour. After a lot of hemming and hawing about which way we were going to go, Slick cleared his throat and hollered to Michael, who was walking back to the pier, "Hey, can we hitch a ride with you guys?"

"Might be another two hours," Michael called back. "We've got a couple of pieces of equipment to check out."

I was ready to wait, but Freddy clicked his fingers, ordering us to move, and we fell into a tight, ten-legged clump heading under the elevated highway for West Street. Less than halfway there, a series of "*Ca-wa-woo's*" echoed ahead of us.

I didn't need J.D. to tell me. Those were not pigeons.

"How far away you figure they are?" Freddy whispered to George.

"A block. Two at the most."

I swear, even at the risk of being branded a yellow belly for life, I would've made a run for it back to the pier if Slick hadn't wrenched my arm just then. "Look what's coming," he cried, crossing himself and kissing a medal around his neck. "It's a cab!"

"Fool. The light's off. Somebody's in it," George muttered.

"So what, man," said J.D. "It's gotta turn one way or other when it gets to West Street. When it breaks, we'll hop on the hood."

"I'm game," I said. "It'd sure outfox the Piranhas. They'll be wondering all night what happened to us."

Freddy's mouth curled and he let out a laugh as

deep and powerful as a Great Dane's bark. "Yeah—
yeah. That's it. The joke's on them."

All five of us took off in a mad dash, reaching West
Street just as two huge oil trucks came rumbling down
the south lane at full speed. We stopped, letting the
first one pass, then tried cutting across the street in
front of the next truck. "Back! Back! Get back!" Freddy
shouted.

We all leaped out of the truck's path, just missing
getting mowed down by a hairsbreadth. As it rumbled
on by, blocking our view of the cab, George called it
every name in the book.

"Holy sheez—we're in luck," J.D. hollered when we
could see the cab again. "Somebody's getting out.
Pffwhee," he whistled. *"Hey, cabbie—wait, man!
Wait!"*

All of us tore across the street, shouting at the top
of our lungs. As soon as the cabbie poked his head
out his window and saw us coming, he turned on his
Off Duty sign and squealed off.

"Ya big priss! Ya nearly knocked me flat on my
rump!" the passenger yelled after him. It was Webber.

FOURTEEN

"PRETTY CRAFTY detective work, eh?"

Webber was beaming, pleased as anything he'd tracked us down. "I must've made a hundred phone calls—mostly to Cruz's," he told Freddy when we whisked him across the street. "Don't you Espaneeolas have any other surnames?"

"*Ca-wa-woo-wa-eeee aw aw!*"

The call seemed to ricochet around us, then echo back from the beams under the highway. We stood petrified under a streetlight, too scared to move. Webber hadn't noticed we'd stopped breathing. "No sireebob," he went on happily. "No point in staying home alone. Not when I can be out painting the town."

"*Ca-wa-woo-wa-eeee aw aw!*"

George's gray face tightened around his darting eyes. "They got a sentinel posted on Clarkson Street," he whispered. "Let's get the hell away from this light."

Everybody set off like shots, turning the corner to run down Morton Street. I grabbed Webber's wrist, dragging him puffing and panting behind me. "What's going on? What's the big hurry?" he asked when we slowed down. I was watching Freddy calculating our next move. He looked around, then motioned for us to keep going straight.

"C'mon, I'll tell you later," I said to Webber, snatching his wrist again.

An old tan and brown sedan, stripped of its back wheels and jacked up on cinder blocks, was sitting in a driveway three quarters of the way down the first block. George and J.D. crept cautiously up to the side and peeked in the windows while Slick edged up to the front and checked under the open hood. "Engine's gone," Slick said.

"*So?*" George was annoyed. "Who's looking for engines?"

Freddy clicked his fingers. "Let's beat it. The coast is clear."

We took off again, running in pairs, Webber and me in the rear, tagging behind J.D. and Slick. "This how you guys get your Saturday night kicks?" Webber asked, tickled pink.

"Watch it," I said, jerking his arm to keep him from tripping over an enormous cake of plaster on the sidewalk.

His belly bounced as he hopped around it. "How long we gonna jog? All night?"

"If we have to," I said. "We've got Piranhas on our trail. J.D. thinks they're out to kill us."

"*Ai-yai-yai,*" he whimpered. "*Ai-yaiiii.*"

A few feet ahead of us, Freddy was holding up his hand. We all slowed down, practically tiptoeing up to the corner of Morton and Washington. Except for a rat scurrying into a sewer drain, Washington Street was deserted, and we bolted across.

On the other side, the streetlight was out. It was hard to see, but we could make out a ramshackle wooden garage on the corner, then a row of crumbling four-story brick tenements with cracked stoops and boarded-up windows. Beyond the tenements, light was streaming out from the ground floor of a tacky-looking warehouse.

We streaked ahead, making it past the last tenement, when an ear-splitting whistle rang out behind us. Freddy and George ducked around the entrance of the warehouse, crouching behind a row of garbage cans lined up under an open window. *"Ggggg-rrrrrr!"* Two evil-looking Dobermans banged against the grille covering the window, then began poking their noses through the iron bars.

"Gggggggggg-rrrrrrrrr!"

The rest of us dashed into the street and squeezed in between a shiny black Buick and an old gray sedan, the only cars parked on the block.

"Ca-wa-waoooo-eee aich aich!"

"Holy sheez," J.D. croaked. "That came from the other way near Greenwich Street. They got scouts everywhere!"

Freddy looked up and the dogs in the warehouse rammed their heads through the grille bars, snapping at his scalp.

Webber was stifling a sob, and Slick, next to me, was quaking so hard he felt like a power lawnmower.

"We're good as dead," he repeated over and over, clutching his medal.

We couldn't go up the street. Or down. If we stayed wedged between the car bumpers, we wouldn't even be able to put up a good fight when the Piranhas closed in on us. Not that I actually pictured myself putting up a good fight—or a bad one either, for that matter. I like having options.

Think, think, I told myself. Was there a good hiding place anywhere? I squinted, trying to see if there was an opening under the stoop of the last tenement house. Crap! Locked gates and no crawl space above or below! My eyes shifted back to the warehouse. Then it hit me. "Come on," I said, squirming to get out from between the cars, "four empty garbage cans! We can get inside them."

Webber's fleshy face puckered. "I won't fit."

"Ca-wa-ooo . . . wa-ooo . . . wa-ooo!" The calls were getting closer.

J.D. hopped over the back fender of the gray car. "Maybe one of the cars is open," he said, doing a running crouch back to the black Buick to check doors. "Sheez. Tighter'n clams. Hey, wait, man—a window's open. C'mon, Webber—I'll hide on the floor with ya."

Webber timidly tiptoed out from between the cars, snagging his checkered pants on a license plate in the process. "My good ones," he said, sniffing, as he got on the floor of the Buick behind J.D.

Another piercing whistle rang out in the distance. No time to lose. Slick and I ran to the cans, panicked. By now the Dobermans were frenzied, rattling the grille bars loose with their thrusts. We grabbed the cans on the end away from the window. Freddy and George were already inside the others.

"Quick," Slick whispered. "Somebody's comin'!"

I made a dive for my can, not noticing the stench till I was knee-deep in a mound of slime. Watery cottage cheese dripped from the lid when I pulled it over my head. Then I gagged as strands of cold spaghetti slithered down my neck. At the same moment I heard the Piranhas come by.

They were talking fast, excited. Hard as I tried, I couldn't make out every word. The Dobermans' snarling had reached a maniacal pitch.

"Ehh, ya lousy mutts," said a raspy voice. "Eat dese."

Ping ping ping ping. Something sounding like pellets hit the grille. Probably strychnine. Smart, those Piranhas. Vicious maybe, but smart. The dogs were quiet.

A lot of mumbling and prowling was going on around the cans. "Wait'll ah git them punks," one guy said as he sat on my lid, bulging it in. "Ahm gonna knock their heads ta bloody stumps—then ahm gonna knock the stumps off."

"Hey, Stab, anybody checked between them cars?"

"Yeah," said another voice.

"Waddabout under 'em?"

"Turtle's doin' it."

"Doors locked?"

"Yeah, 'n the windows is rolled up. Can't see nuttin'."

"*Gggggggg-rrrrrrrrrrrrrrrr!*" The dogs were reviving.

"Shudup da mutts, Cannibal."

"Can't," said the guy sitting on my lid. "Outta M & M's."

"Here, catch. Give 'em pretzels."

Plub-bunk. The bulge snapped up, relieving the pressure on the top of my head. *Ping ping ping ping.* Quiet again. Those faking Dobermans.

Sweat was pouring down my face and neck, mingling with coffee grounds and bits of decaying orange rind. Air—air. I had to get air.

Without jarring the can, I carefully ran my hands around the inside surface, hoping to find a hole. Pain was shooting through my cramped knees. It got so bad, finally, I had to quit searching for oxygen and concentrate on shifting my legs. *Ouch!*

Something sharp was cutting into my shin. A gash in the can maybe? I felt under my leg. Blast it!— nothing but a bottle cap.

"Anybody try the gates under them stoops?"

"Yeah. Checked every blinkin' one a them the whole block," said a new voice. "Any a youse guys try them trapdoors?"

What trapdoors? I hadn't seen any!

"Where?" asked Cannibal.

"Idiot! Underneat ya. They go to the warehouse cellar."

Cannibal let out a loud roar, then there was a terrible crashing and clanking—like an elephant having a tantrum.

"If them doors don't give for *me*," he said with a wicked laugh, "they don't give for nobody!"

Plub-bunk. He was back on my lid, weighing down

on my skull again. Now I was getting a kink in my neck. What next? I rotated my head slightly, ripping my cheek across a jagged object. Something warm trickled down my chin. *Blood?*

I reached behind my ear, probing around with one finger to find out what'd ripped me. Instead of losing my finger on a razor blade like I expected, it slipped through a hole the size of a quarter and came out the other side of the can, poking Cannibal's leg. His hand came down, swatting my finger like it was a fly. I quickly jerked it back through the hole, skinning it on the sharp, curled edge.

An air hole! Now if I could only get my nose in front of it.

"Anybody checked out them cans?" came the voice I now recognized as Stab's.

"Naww. Only morons'd hide in 'em," said Cannibal.

"Waddya think the Falcons is? Check, Man!"

Cannibal hopped off my lid. "Hokay . . . ya say so."

My heart was pounding double time. Was it possible, I wondered, for someone to O.D. on his own adrenaline? I hoped so. I wanted to be unconscious when Cannibal found me.

"Ppppfeeeeeeeiiewwww!" he gasped, prying the lid open a couple of inches, then slamming it shut again. "Ea-acchh! Whatever's in there, man—ya gotta know it's been dead a week. Ah ain't checkin' the others. You wanna, you do it."

"Ehh. Skip 'em. Damn it all anyway—they're here! I know it. I seen 'em."

Another shrill whistle blasted the air. "Who ya figger

that is?" somebody asked, surprised. "Ain't none a the
Piranhas I posted on the corner."

"Wart-Hogs?"

"Falcons; maybe?"

"C'mon," roared Cannibal. "Let's git 'em. Let's gouge
out their eyes 'n' spit in the sockets!"

Their sneakers padded down the pavement, grad-
ually fading from earshot. I was drained. Limp as an
old string mop. Soon as I heard movement in the next
can, I pounded my head against the lid of mine, trying
to loosen it. "Thought ya said these things was empty,"
Slick was whining.

"Sshhh! Shut up," Freddy called from inside his can.
"Somebody's comin' outta the cellar."

Slick's lid clanked down again just as mine sprang
loose, toppling from my head, then rattle-banging
onto the pavement. I made a grab for it, but it'd
already bounced out of reach, veered once, and started
rolling for the gutter. "What the—Good God! *Horace!*"
a man yelled. "That *you*, kid?"

Light from the cellar was flooding the pavements,
and I looked over to where the trapdoors were flapped
open. "*Jake?*" I said meekly.

"Say, what the blazes is going on out here?" another
voice said.

A night watchman was standing on the warehouse
steps, restraining the gnashing, snarling Dobermans.
"You," he shouted. "You in the garbage! You the one
throwing candy at my hounds?"

Jake climbed out of the cellar followed by a woman
with lots of yellow hair and a mouthful of gum. "It's

nothing, Charlie," he said, waving his hand to dismiss the watchman. "Just my brother's kid, okay? Take the killers inside."

"Sorry, Mr. Hobart. Didn't know." The watchman shrugged, guiding the dogs back in the warehouse. Both were wagging their stumpy tails. They knew Jake.

The woman looked at me, popping her gum. "That there's your *nephew?*"

"Go to the car, Goldie!" Jake sounded irritated.

"Thanks for calling off the dogs, Jake. I—"

"God!" he yelled, cutting me off. "What'd you do to your eye?" His face was screwed up like he was in pain. Suddenly he dropped the heavy metal trapdoors, letting them crash open on the cement. A tremor ran through the ground. "Barney didn't say—"

"Aw, it's nothing. Really," I said as he charged over to me.

"Lemme see," he said, squatting down so we were face to face over the rim of the garbage can. "Nothing, huh?" He poked at my eyepatch. "Then why're you wearing *that?*"

"Low-grade infection," I whispered.

He shook his head. "God, what a sight. Flo's gonna have a rigor when you get home."

"Why? Am I still bleeding?"

"Uh-uh. But you're sure covered with marinara sauce. Here, use this," he said, pulling a hanky out of his pocket. As I wiped, he bombarded me with questions: What was I doing there . . . was I crazy . . . didn't I know what a seamy neighborhood it was?

And who was I hiding from? And why were they chasing me anyhow? Was I alone?

I picked coffee grounds out of my ears and nose, telling him about the movie and the Piranhas. Things seemed quiet when I finished. "Wanna come out now?" I said, knocking on Slick's can. Jake helped me out of mine and looked sick watching me scrape a mushed, rotten melon off my shoe. "Freddy? George?" I called. "It's safe. My uncle's here. By the way, why're you in town, Jake? You're supposed to be in Chicago."

"Change of plans," he said abruptly.

I glanced at the flaking sign over the warehouse door. CONSOLIDATED RICE CO., INC. "But I thought your business place was in New Jersey?"

"This is a subsidiary. Sorta secret . . . know what I mean, kid. Never saw you tonight. Okay?"

"Fine with me, Jake." Both of us turned and watched the three garbage can lids rise, millimeter by millimeter. "My buddies," I said when faces appeared. "Freddy on the end there, then George and Slick. Guys, my uncle . . . Jake Hobart, and that's . . ." I glanced at the woman, sitting on the fender of his black Buick.

"My business associate," Jake finished quickly.

Freddy, Slick, and George, jumpy as polecats, climbed out of their cans, flicking off garbage and mumbling, "Pleezameetcha."

"Yeah, pleasure's mine, I'm sure," said Jake. "Now all four of you beat it on home while nobod—"

Wheeeeeeeee-zeeeeeeeeeeeeeeeeet!! Wheeeeeeeeee-eeeee-zeeeeeeeeeeeeeeeeeet!!

Freddy's eyes narrowed. "Back in the—"

"Naw, get down there," Jake ordered, shooing us away from the cans and down the cellar steps.

It sounded like all hell was breaking loose less than a block away. Pops, bangs, explosions—with whistle blasts for background music. The Fourth of July gone crazy! Jake hopped down the steps, asking if the gang on our trail was Oriental. "No? Well, the one coming is—been here before. Damned near demolished the neighborhood. Hear that?—a cherry bomb! Take this," he said, pressing a key in my hand. "They're gonna skin you alive if you don't get out the back way."

A split second after he'd shot off instructions on how we could get to a "friend's" place by going through the cellar and across the courtyard in back, a wild, screeching, screaming stampede started up the block toward us.

Jake hopped up to the sidewalk, lowering the trap-doors over our heads. "Got everything I said?" he called down. "Cuz once I lock these you can't get out this way. Go out the back, lock up with your key, and hands up if the big galoot over there pulls anything on ya. Give him the password, then ask for Mickey. Okay? Be talkin' with ya, kid," he said through the crack. "And remember—*no lights!*"

We heard a bolt click, tumbling into place, then whooping and hollering and war cries and firecrackers. We quickly groped our way along a damp, musty corridor, feeling for the barricade of rice bags Jake had told us would be blocking the door to the back room.

"Think I found 'em," Freddy whispered.

On the street a car squealed, taking off. "There goes Jake," I said.

Then we all realized we'd forgotten J.D. and Webber.

FIFTEEN

"GOING TO *Hoboken*?—but that's in *Jersey*!"

Slick let out a whistle, then nobody said anything for the longest time. "S'pose it coulda been worse," Freddy finally said, ending the silence. "Ace's uncle could live in Philly."

We were sealed in the pitch black cellar with a wild melée of cherry bombs exploding right above us, and Jake's car had already left anyway, so there wasn't anything we could do to rescue J.D. and Webber.

We all huddled next to Freddy, feeling the barricade of rice bags he'd found. From what I could tell from running my hands around them, there were hundreds of heavy bags packed tight from the floor to the ceiling. Our next job was to locate the stack in the center that rolled out on a dolly. "Fifteen to the right," Jake had said, "then pull." I counted. "Somebody get down at the bottom," I whispered. "A wheel oughta be by my foot."

We all tugged, grunting. Then there was a deep, rumbling groan like a whole house shifting. The moveable wall of bags on the dolly slid forward and I slipped behind it, feeling for the door to the back room. I found it, opened it, and stepped inside, sinking ankle-deep into carpet bouncy enough to be a moss bed. "C'mon," I said.

The three of them squeezed in after me, and we rolled the dolly back in place. "Cuckoo warehouse, ain't it?" said Slick.

The cigar smoke in the back room was so heavy and pungent it could have been bottled. I inched forward, plugging my nose, and stumbled right into a huge table. When I put my hands down to steady myself, I felt poker chips and dice.

"This here Jake your uncle that's the gangster?" George asked.

"Well, uh—he says he went straight and he's a wholesale rice distributor," I said, "but I, uh—think it's a cover-up."

"Better believe it! Listen to this." George sounded like he was a couple of feet to my right, and something near him whirred like it was spinning. Then a ball rolled. "Hear that?—a roulette wheel."

My curiosity was getting the best of me. Matches. Where'd I felt them?—by the ashtray? I slid my fingers across the fuzzy tabletop. There. Found a box of them. "No harm in a little peek," I said striking a half dozen matches.

All of us sucked in our breath, looking around. Plush scarlet carpeting. Paneled walls with oil paintings. Soundproof ceiling. Blackjack, roulette, and crap tables—another table under a crystal chandelier for cards! Whew. A regular casino.

"Betcha I know who's linked up with a mob," said George.

Freddy was nervous. "C'mon, the door's backa the blackjack table. Let's beat it!"

I blew out the torch in my hand. No wonder Jake had insisted on lights out. "Nobody saw anything, right?" I said when we went out the door.

"Right," they echoed.

I locked up and we started creeping across the courtyard in back, looking for the rear entrance to the building on the other side. For a couple of minutes inside the soundproof room we'd forgotten all about the gangs of butchers looking for us.

Awful shrieks and screaming and yelling were still going on it front of the warehouse. We heard a bunch of firecrackers go off in another part of the neighborhood, then a bloodcurdling cry. "Coulda been one a us," said Slick.

"Yeah," I said.

"*Stop! Who goes?*" A hulking giant with a squashed-in face moved out from the shadows of the courtyard, pointing a snub-nosed pistol at us.

Our hands shot up in the air and George nudged me, telling me to give him the password. "Uhhh—Humpty-Dumpty," I said. "We're looking for Mickey."

Squash Face lowered his pistol and mumbled something into a walkie-talkie. He waited a second for an answer, got one, then herded us in front of a metal door that slid sideways, exposing the interior of an elevator. "Buzz one," he said, motioning for us to get inside.

We did, and when we stepped out on the next floor

a tiny pale guy was waiting for us. *"Mickey?"* asked my foghorn.

"Yes," he answered with a lisp. "And you?"

"Ace. Ace Hobart. Jake Hobart's nephew. He—um, Jake, that is—sent us. Said you could get us a ride uptown."

Mickey gave us the once-over, smiling, but his nose was turned up, sniffing the garbage on us. "Don't you have something to give me?" he asked sweetly.

He wasn't nearly as sweet as he looked. The whole time I was searching my jeans for Jake's key, he had his hand in his pocket, holding a gun on me. *Where the heck had I put it?*

"Here," I said, realizing I had the key in my hand.

He took it, still smiling, then led us into a claustrophobic little room where he told us to sit on the bench and wait. He left, locking us in, and was back a couple of minutes later with a guy in a gray uniform. "Take these boys home, Dimitri."

"Right boss. Where they going?"

"One stop'll do it," said Freddy. "Just drop us all off on the corner of Twenty-third and Eighth."

This new guy, Dimitri, looked at him with watery eyes that had no expression. "You'll go to your own places unless the boss says otherwise," he said in a hoarse voice. "Here—write down your addresses."

He passed us a little pad and pencil from his pocket and we all wrote. I sort of didn't want him to have my address, he was so creepy, so I just wrote corner of Twenty-third and First. It was near Raven's. If it wasn't too late, I'd call.

"Hurry, *boys*—I have things to attend to," said Mickey.

Dimitri grabbed the pad away from Slick.

"Hey, I ain't finished yet."

Dimitri ignored him and ushered us out of the room, around the corner, and through some drapes hanging over an entrance to a short hall. At the end of the hall there was a door going into a dimly lit living room— wallpaper, Venetian blinds, and everything. Somebody nearby was crying softly and the room smelled funny —like flowers and melted wax. Outside on the street, all kinds of whooping and hollering and battling was going on, so we knew the Piranhas and Monsoons were still at it. I winced when I heard a vicious roar followed by a high, endless squeal of pain. "Cannibal's gouging somebody's eyes out," I whispered. The others nodded.

We hurried through the living room, nobody talking, and past a narrow alcove filled with burning candles. Inside it, a dead man was laid out in a coffin. Wreaths and stands of gladiolus were flanking the sides, and a woman in black was sitting in a chair with her face buried in a hanky.

Slick crossed himself, praying, as we filed out a door and went down some steps into a garage jammed with limousines and hearses. "I ain't ridin' in no hearse," he said when Dimitri opened the back end of one for us.

"Get in!" said Dimitri.

He wasn't the kind of guy you argued with. Still, I think we would've made a fuss if a cherry bomb hadn't exploded close to the garage doors. My ears were ringing, but I clawed my way into the hearse right behind Slick.

As soon as Freddy and George got in, Dimitri hurried up front to the driver's seat and started the engine.

From the little we could see through the pleated gray curtains on the windows, the garage door opened automatically and the lights went out. Then the hearse shot out into the darkness like a torpedo. In every direction, there were guys mopping up the streets with each other.

One big bruiser about double the size of Mean Joe Greene flew out of the path of the hearse's squealing tires, cradling a foot in his hands like it'd been creamed. He was roaring and bawling louder than a wounded grizzly, and I pressed my head against the window to see him better, wondering if he was Cannibal.

The tires squealed again. We made a turn that hurled us into one side of the hearse, then another that flung us the other way. Freddy quickly scrambled to the back curtains, taking a peek at the fighting on the corner. "Look at 'em," he said. "Man, if that ain't a massacre, I never seen one before."

Bats, sticks, firecrackers—fists! Whew. I'd never had any idea there were so *many* Piranhas and Monsoons. Fifty, maybe. We were down the street now, stopped at a light, and I kept worrying that somehow they'd sense us. Freddy, next to me, swallowed like he had a big, hard rock in his throat.

"I'd like to get out and smash some skulls myself," he said as we peeled across the intersection.

"Yeah," George growled. "We could pin 'em to the sidewalks and do a jig on 'em."

Slick didn't say anything until we were uptown, zooming along Twenty-third Street. "Poor stiff back in the funeral parlor," he said, cracking his knuckles. "What a way to end up."

For some reason that made me think of J.D. and Webber. In a few minutes we'd be home safe and sound in our beds. But what about them? Where were they? I hoped Jake and his business associate, Goldie, hadn't gotten too mad when they found them hiding in the car—kicked them out and made them walk home or anything.

Dimitri stopped at my corner first and came around and opened the rear of the hearse. "Thanks," I said as I hopped out. But he didn't respond.

"Rest in peace," George called after me.

"Cut out the crap!" Freddy said irritably. "See ya at six A.M. Monday, Ace."

I waved, watching the red taillights disappear down the street, then looked at the clock in the window of the cleaners on the corner. Ten to twelve. I was all hyped up and wanted to talk—tell somebody about all the action I'd seen—but it was too late to call Raven. Maybe I could leave her a note.

For fifty cents a guy at a newspaper stand sold me a brown paper bag and lent me his ballpoint.

"Dear Raven," I wrote on the bag,

> Wish you could have been on the waterfront with us. The moon was pretty—no bigger than a little toenail clipping . . .

I tore up the bag. That had sounded better when Freddy had said it. "Can I have another bag?" I asked the newspaper guy.

"Sure. Only forty cents for a second one."

"Dear Raven," I began again,

> We had a little trouble with the Piranhas and Monsoons coming home from the shooting. Nothing we couldn't handle though. Really. My cheek got gashed, but don't worry, it'll heal. . . .

I felt my cut and looked at the newspaper guy. "Is it bad?" I asked.

"Is what bad?"

"Oh, never mind."

"In fact, forget I even mentioned it," I continued in my note. I signed it, then added:

> P.S. If you can, watch the This Morning show on Monday. It'll be the first appearance of a new household word.

I gave the guy back his pen and folded the bag so I could slip it in Raven's mailbox. "You been sick?" the guy asked me as I started to walk away.

My fingers went to my patch. "This? Naw. Happened a long time ago."

"That isn't what I meant," he said, looking at my arms.

I looked down at the spaghetti and cottage cheese stuck to the hairs. "Here, kid, take these," he said, handing me a package of tissues. "Better clean your-self up before you go home."

I took out some tissues and picked at my skin as I walked away. "Hey—you think those are *free*?" he yelled. I paid him and started down the street toward Raven's building. The drunk who'd told me how to get to the pier was curled up in a doorway, snoring, and sirens were wailing in the distance. I sighed. Nothing like the sights and sounds of the jungle.

SIXTEEN

SUNDAY WAS a void. A blank. A day blipped off the calendar and out of my life. Gone. Stamped CAN-CELED.

Blurry, sketchy memories, that's all I have of it. One was waking up late, close to noon, feeling something cold—a mirror?—under my nose and hearing Nora shouting, "It's fogging up, Mom. He's not dead."

Then I must have dozed off again, dreaming of Raven, kissing . . .

But paradise can't last forever. Not in The Pits, anyway. Eventually Mom made me get up to eat, and I know I did, but I can't recall what exactly. At the time I was a lot more interested in the news. Something Dad was reading. "Police ought to stay out of these wars," he was saying behind his paper. "If these guys want to do themselves in, let 'em. Get rid of a few. City'd be—"

Was I so groggy I wasn't hearing right? "A war—in New York?" I asked.

"If that's what you want to call a bunch of punks

making mincemeat out of each other," he said, folding the front page so everybody at the table could see:

ALL-OUT GANG WAR NEAR WATERFRONT
Twenty-three members of five youth gangs are being treated for injuries sustained . . .

Five gangs? My eyes shifted down the column, quickly skimming for names. Nothing. They weren't listed. The Piranhas and Monsoons had to be two— the Wart-Hogs probably the third. But who the heck were the other two?

Whatever it was I can't remember eating fell out of my hands. The sirens I'd heard! They must've been police cars and ambulances.

"Anybody killed?" asked Nora, the gore freak.

"Who? These brutes?" Dad roared. "You kidding? They got a whole army of doctors doing handstands, getting them better. They'll be back on the streets before they know what hit them!"

Back on the streets? My tongue was dry and I could feel my knees bounce up and down, up and down— out of control.

"What gets me more than anything," Dad ranted on, "is all the beds they're using. Hospitals everywhere. St. Vincent's. Beth Israel, Bellevue. But if anybody *we* knew got run over, there wouldn't be . . ."

"Calm down, Barney," Mom said, slicing him a wedge of something or other.

"*I am calm!* And I tell you, Flo, it's a disgrace!"

About that time Mom started noticing how "gray" I

looked. "What'd they feed you at that party you went to last night, Horace?"

"Not much," I said. "Sandwiches, pickles, cole slaw, spaghetti, baked beans," making up a menu, "cheese, bananas, cakes . . ."

"That could be it. Gorging on rich foods. That or the vent."

"Probably the food," I said. "I feel kind of barfy."

"Then you're going right back to bed!" she said, helping me up like I was six instead of sixteen. "And you're staying there the rest of the day."

I let my mouth droop slightly, so I looked worse. I didn't want to talk to anybody *or* think. Crawling into the sack and escaping into sleep was what I needed. I was out again within minutes, and didn't wake up till hours later when Mom brought me some soup.

"Jake called this afternoon," she said, setting the tray on my bed. "Nothing in particular. He's back from Chicago and just wanted to know how we all were. I told him fine, except you had a little stomach-ache. He said to tell you he was sorry and say hello."

"That's *all*?" I asked.

She thought a moment. "There was something else—something he told your dad. Oh, I remember. Coming home from the airport last night, he met a couple of your friends near the Holland Tunnel and gave them a lift. Isn't that a strange coincidence?" she said, laughing.

"Yeah. Real strange. Where'd he take them?"

"Home. Both of them—drove them all the way into Manhattan. Nice of him, wasn't it?"

After she left, I lay there awhile, wishing I could call Webber and J.D. to find out what happened, see how they were. But that was impossible. I'd have to wait until tomorrow morn—*tomorrow morning*! The TV studio. I'd almost forgotten. Six. Six in the darned A.M.! What kind of excuse was I going to use to get out of here at that hour? And what about the folks? I couldn't chance letting them be my audience for the *This Morning* show.

I'd have to deactivate the TV set. Pull a tube— jimmy the switch. Something. Then sneak out—leave a note. Mention an early-morning math-review workshop. That ought to do it. I should have been going to one.

Back to sleep, I told myself, closing my eyes. I was really developing my faculty for inventing excuses. Nearly as good as Nevada Culhane, I thought, grinning. Then my eyes flew open. Those other two gangs! Dad said they'd be back on the streets. Would they?

And where'd they come from, anyway?

SEVENTEEN

"JEEZ, MAN," J.D. was saying, "who you think they *are*?"

"Yeah, what's their turf?" asked Slick.

"Don't know. Papers didn't give no names," said Freddy.

I was the last one at the NBS studio building and found the Falcons waiting for me by the lobby elevator. "Who you talking about—those other two gangs Saturday?" I asked, slapping J.D. five when he stuck out his hand. I was glad Jake had taken care of him.

"You got any idea where they're from?" George asked me.

"*Me*? No. None," I said, taking the jacket with the giant ant Freddy handed me. It was a mile too big across the shoulders, but I put it on anyway. "Why, don't *you* know?" I asked George. I'd gotten so I expected him to know everything.

"Nobody here does," he said, stepping into the elevator when the doors opened. He pressed twenty-five after we all crowded in after him, then looked at

Freddy who was chewing on an inside corner of his mouth. "What about your brother?" he asked. "Didn't his feelers come up with anything?"

Freddy spit out a piece of skin. "Nuttin' much. Opinions is all. They think maybe they're undergrounders."

"Yeah, could be," said George. "Could be they're *imported* undergrounders—places like Hackensack or Newark."

J.D. scratched his neck like he had hives. "What's gonna happen when they get outta the hospital?"

"C'mon, don't talk about it," whined Slick. "I'm gonna forget what I was gonna say on TV."

All of us looked at him and shut up. The elevator doors were opening. Directly across the hall was NBS.

"You're ten minutes late!" snapped a woman with a clipboard who was waiting for us. She whipped us through the reception area, then in and out of the makeup room faster than you could say spit. When that was finished, she rushed us around the corner to some double doors with a red light over them. "Quiet!" she whispered.

We followed her into the studio, walking like flamingoes on grass, raising our feet high so we wouldn't trip on the cables strewn all over the floor. The place was huge with maps and blowups of cityscapes on the walls. Up front I got my first in-the-flesh glimpse at Dean Willit and Charlotte Van Dyne.

Freddy jabbed me in the side, staring at Charlotte. "She's even sexier real than on TV!"

I nodded but kept quiet because the woman with

the clipboard shot us a dirty look. "This way," she said, leading us toward a circle of sleek-looking chairs in an area marked INTERVIEWS. The chairs were surrounded by spotlights on high stands.

"Three minutes!" a voice called over a mike. Charlotte and Willit were talking to each other. We sat down, not saying anything, and the woman we'd been following picked up some mikes and hooked one around each of our necks. "Tap them, okay?" She leaned forward and flipped mine with her fingernail. "Hear that? It's alive."

Seconds ticked slowly by. I was worrying about what they'd ask and what we'd say.

Suddenly the lights around us blazed. Freddy and I turned to each other. I could see every pore and blackhead on his face. Slick looked like he might throw up. J.D. slammed his feet against the base of his chair like somebody was going to work him over right there. George shifted and his chair groaned. "This is it!" he said for everyone.

Charlotte and Dean Willit came forward and asked us our names, memorizing them by pointing to each of us and saying them. They checked their notes and she, in a get-on-with-it voice, said, "Who's the star of the movie?"

I couldn't get the words out, so George said, "Ace here."

"Oh—*Ace*? You mean Horasis?" She bit her lip. "You talk about it, Ace? The patch?" She shrugged, waffling her hand. "Don't have to."

I opened my hands as if it didn't matter.

"Just relax and listen," Willit said. "We won't ask

anything too hard. Be thinking what *you'd* like to tell the audience. We're going to ask what you feel is important to teenagers in New York. Think of it as a chance to make a statement, to let people *out there* know what it's really like to be a *kid now*. One thing! Remember, don't talk unless you're asked a question or I signal you to join in. If you want to speak out, wiggle your finger like this. Okay?"

"Okay," we said in unison.

"That's all the instructions?" George said.

Willit and Charlotte looked bland. "Nothing to it," they said.

"Be yourselves," she said.

"Heh-heh," went J.D. Freddy wheeled around like he was going to slug him.

The stars took the two seats facing us. The lights were adjusted by the crew and the cameras came in close. After a lead-in commercial and the weather report, Willit nodded to us and began to talk.

"Today on *This Morning* we have the young actors from *Bound and Gagged*, a movie that will graphically depict the violence that all too often erupts between teenagers on our streets and in our parks. Here's *Ace Hobart*—Horasis Hobart—a star of *Bound and Gagged*, a soon-to-be-released film. Hello, Ace."

"Hello, Mr. Willit."

"Where are you from, Ace?"

"Uh—from New York City now—but I was from Guttenberg."

"And where's that?" Mr. Willit asked. "Where they translated the Bible into the vernacular?"

"New Jersey—twenty-five minutes from the bridge."

"I knew it!" Slick whispered.

"Cool it!" Freddy snapped under his breath.

The camera moved to pick him up. "Sorry—was nuttin'." My heart sank, we were going to bomb.

Willit said, "This is *Freddy Cruz*, leader of the Purple Falcons, a gang from Kennedy High in Manhattan. We know there was a serious gang fight Saturday night near the docks. As a result, twenty-three young men were in the emergency rooms of three New York hospitals and thirteen of them were hospitalized for injuries afterward. Freddy Cruz, could you tell us anything about the incident? Would a gang from Kennedy, for instance, be involved with something like this in that location?"

"No, Mr. Willit. You see, everybody's got his turf." He sounded just like the big shot on the seven o'clock news. "The Falcons' turf is Eighth between Twenty-first Street and Fourteenth—and some blocks east and west, depending. But the Falcons don't mess around the docks, see? However, by coincidence, the night of that unfortunate action the Falcons were down there because of the movie we're makin' for the Maroons. But, of course, we didn't see those guys which ended up in St. Vincent's—we were driven home in a private —*car*." He glanced at the rest of us and we all shook our heads.

"And, um, what do you Falcons do *after* school, on your leisure time?" Willit said, looking at J.D. I held my breath.

J.D. shrugged. "Just like other kids," he said after a while. "A little hustle now and then—know what I

mean? Conditions being what they are now with infla-
tion and so on—lots of people out of work need money
—so sometimes we hustle. Of course, it's not easy, the
cops makin' up all these new laws now and keepin'
people from doing anything much—"

"How would you answer this, *Slick?*"

"The Falcons have given up rippin' off parked cars,
muggin', and gang wars, so all's left is pool, and J.D.
here frazzles—*dances.*"

I coughed, trying to drown out the *ka-pow, ka-pow*
of my heart.

George said, "It's not as bad as everybody in the
media would have ya think. A lot of so-called rough-
ness is just a cover—know what I mean? A lot of it's
for guys who're scared."

"Oh, you're saying then—" Charlotte broke in.

Willit interrupted her with: "But kids were honestly
hurt in the melee Saturday night, weren't they?"

George said, "Looked like it from the papers, but
maybe the publishers are just trying to do a little
hustle themselves—sell a few extra papers—who
knows? Ya gotta know your sources."

"Do you mean *sometimes* some of the tough guys
are putting on an act?" Charlotte said, looking bright
and interested.

"Well, you gotta act tough, right? Because the other
guys may *really* be tough, right? So that's it. It's more
actin' than real sometimes. I don't see too much to
worry about."

Charlotte said, "You don't?"

"Some places maybe—not here."

Charlotte laughed lightly. "I hope you're right."

"You're all members of the same gang then?" Willit asked quickly.

The camera took in Slick. "All of us are Falcons."

"But aren't you kind of an unusual group? I mean you're a *mixture* of backgrounds and races—"

"Yeah, but that doesn't matter. It's what's inside that counts," George said, patting his chest. "That's what holds the group together, y'know?"

"We're birds of a feather," Freddy said.

"Yeah!" Slick said. "You know the old saying, Charlotte. Birds of a feather . . . *falcon* together."

J.D. looked at him and started to laugh.

Freddy glared at him. It was getting hotter than bee spit under the lights.

"Sorry!" J.D. said, shutting his mouth firmly.

Charlotte said, "Violence is part of your lives—the movie's accurate in that, isn't it? I mean, you Falcons know about mugging and ripping off and—" She was looking at me, smiling softly, as if she were asking about our classes.

I wanted to say I'd joined *after* the Falcons gave up ripping off cars, etc. My foghorn came out and said, "I swear I don't know anything the Falcons have ever done that's illegal. They just know about violence from hearing about it is all, Mrs. Van Dyne. I never saw them do anything. Mrs. Maroon even had to *teach* them how to mug for the movie."

George gave me a look as if he approved; it made me feel good.

"I see. Ace, have you had an accident? I mean, is

your eye injured, perhaps, because of some violence on the streets?" Charlotte asked.

"Uh—well—uh—it's—"

Slick suddenly cleared his throat and broke in, "The cops shot him, Charlotte, is what we think happened."

Her eyes went wide.

"No! That's not it." I thought wildly. "It's a subject that—well, losing eyes maybe ought not to be brought up just now when everybody across America is in the middle of eating breakfast bowls of cereal or eggs or granola or—but you should know it wasn't the *cops*, but—"

I looked at Charlotte, pleading, hoping she'd move on to something else, but she stared back, letting me run on. "A lot of people, you see, don't like somebody who wears a patch. That's right, they don't like a patch wearer, because they worry maybe they're sneaky or don't tell the truth exactly, but once I left Guttenberg, where it was hard going with a patch, I found everything different here. The Falcons didn't let it bother them. They made me their friend right away. The first day! And since then we've been like brothers. They're like a family to me. So good to me—uh—" I was making myself sick with all the schmalz I was saying but I couldn't stop. The Falcons were staring at me with odd expressions, like I was coming unhinged.

"Yeah," Freddy said finally butting in. "We took Ace under our wing—er, wings."

Slick's eyes were shiny. "Birds of a feather, like we said."

"It's okay with us he's only got one eye," George said. "What're friends for? We got no hang-ups about appearances and so on anyway."

"That's right, man. Black or white, rich or poor, smart or dumb—what's it matter? Once a Falcon, always a Falcon, through thick or thin, for richer or poorer—" J.D. said.

"Yeah," everybody said.

"How do you like the movie business?" Willit asked, breaking in.

"Nuttin' wrong with it," Freddy said. We all nodded our heads.

"Doesn't it ever interfere with your homework?" Charlotte asked.

"Homework?" Slick said. "I just skip it."

"How'd you guys get into the movies?" Willit asked.

"Ace was *discovered*," said Freddy. "Then he got us in. We owe it all to him, don't we, guys?"

"Yeah, Ace! Birds of a fea—" Slick said, his face shiny with excitement.

"Dean, I was wondering why Ace's jacket is different from the rest of the guys'." Charlotte said.

"Well," I said, poking my arms out the long sleeves. "My own jacket disappeared Saturday at the shooting. So I had to borrow this, uh—Marab—"

"Marabunta jacket—it's my brother's," Freddy said.

"We only have time now for a word from each of the Falcons. I'd like to hear anything special you'd like to say—a thought you'd like to leave with your listeners," said Charlotte.

George wiggled his finger. "Be nicer to teenagers,

more patient and generous—know what I mean? Listen to their side for once—they deserve it."

"Especially you cops," J.D. broke in.

Slick said, "Don't forget, birds of a—"

Freddy said, "It's not the kids who are bad; it's the world."

"Ace?"

"Ummm—ummm." Nothing came to me, *me*, the *star* of the movie. Suddenly, though, I realized my opportunity. It was worth a try. "If anyone watching knows where my jacket with the dragon embroidered on the back is, please leave me a message at the Riviera Hotel. Thanks."

Charlotte and Willit blinked.

The cameras were rolled back and the lights went off. Dean Willit stood up, waved goodbye, and went back to his desk. Charlotte, grinned, and said, "Thanks, guys."

"Don't think nuttin' of it. *Anytime,*" Freddy said.

As soon as we got in the elevator, we let out a whoop. Then, suddenly, we were all quiet, thinking about what we'd just been through. I wondered about the Falcons—could their toughness really be an act? Did they know how to mug? I felt sort of disappointed —maybe we really were birds of a feather.

George, I noticed, was giving me a funny look.

"What's eatin' ya, George?" Freddy said. The elevator door opened and we got off in the marble lobby.

"It cracks me up, Ace saying something personal like the stuff about his jacket. What's somebody from North Carolina or Iowa going to think of that? Huh?"

"It just came out!" I said.

"Hey, we were good!" J.D. said. "Don't knock him!"

"I thought we was too," Slick said.

"Sensational!" J.D. said, kicking his heels together.

Freddy grinned. "Like newscasters, huh?"

After that even George had to smile. "We didn't blow anything," he said, and then I realized he'd had it all planned. They knew what they were doing.

According to the nasty cabby who drove us down to Kennedy, we were all mean and rotten—a tough gang of hoods. He said as much, so we didn't tip, and when we got out of the taxi nobody shut the doors. The guy, swearing, had to pull over to the curb, get out, and shut them himself.

Reputation intact, we marched into the school like a moving wall.

EIGHTEEN

THE NEWS had hit the school. Everybody knew the Falcons had been on TV and had parts in a movie. Going out for lunch, we were mobbed at the front door by kids who'd steered clear of us any other time. Girls mostly. They were saying, "Hi, Ace!" and "Hey— think you can get me into the flicks?" Stuff like that.

Raven took my arm and dragged me away from my fans so we could reach the rest of the Falcons at the bottom of the steps. George wasn't with them. We waited a few minutes, but the mobs started forming around us again, and Freddy made us break away and head for Mario's. "Maybe he's already there," he said.

He wasn't. Not even inside at the counter or in the john. We looked.

"Okay. Who seen George last?" Freddy asked when we went outside. He was upset.

"Me. In gym, third period—doing chin-ups," said J.D. "He's the champ and everybody was trying to imita—"

"Quiet!" Little red dots were appearing on Freddy's cheeks. "He's never *not* been here for lunch, has he?"

There was a solemn silence.

"You think he's been nabbed?" asked Raven.

"My pal?" said Slick. "Who'd wanna get my pal?"

"You know who!" said Freddy.

Everybody seemed to know except me. Even Slick. "Oh, yeah—the Piranhas," he said, fiddling with his medal.

"But *how?*" I asked. "George was in school! They couldn't just march in there and snatch him right out of—"

The words died in my mouth and there was another long silence. Finally Freddy looked at me, scraping his boot along the cement. "They done it before, Ace. Last year they made off with Little Foxy—nabbed him right after gym."

"Yeah, and he didn't have no clothes on," said Slick. "He was in the shower."

"Oh?" I looked at Raven. It really bothered me that there wasn't anybody around by the name of Little Foxy anymore. "Who is he—er, was he?" I asked.

"One of the Seven Ghouls," she said.

"What are they—the Six Ghouls now?"

"Inmates. They're all in the slammer."

"Wanna order?" the pizza man asked us.

"Naw, we ain't hungry," Freddy said.

"Who isn't?" J.D. asked.

"We aren't," Raven said.

"Oh." I said. J.D. gave me a desperate look.

"Well, let's get back to school and see what happens," said Slick. "Maybe we'll get a message."

"I'll call the Maroons," I offered.

But Marilyn and François hadn't heard anything.

On the phone, Marilyn wanted to talk about the TV show. "Lovey, you need a little training," she said. "Come over after school. I need to give you your first PR lesson. If we hadn't been so busy filming, we'd have thought of it before."

"We gotta find George after school, Marilyn. We'll call you soon as we know something."

"Do that!"

After school Freddy sent us all straight home.

"Keep your lines clear," he said. "Anybody calls about George, phone the message to me right away. I'll contact the others."

"Who do you think is going to call?" J.D. asked for the tenth time.

"I know who's going to call—right, Freddy?" Slick said. "One of the gang members. They must have seen us on TV, right?"

Freddy nodded. "One thing they're good at is communication."

Silence. With George gone, it seemed as if only half of us were here on the street. I wondered if I'd ever see him again. We split up then, Raven going with me.

"Watch out for her!" Freddy said, the last thing.

"Sure!" I said in my foghorn, but inside I was shaking. Suppose we ran into the Piranhas or the Wart-Hogs on the street—the ones who weren't in the hospital? Would I run? I saw Raven up to the door of her apartment. I didn't want anybody surprising her on the stairs.

"Want to come in, Ace? I'm starving," she said. "We've got some Fritos."

"Naw, better not. I want to get home, like Freddy

said. See you later. Don't forget to call if you need me."

"Say it that way and I'll call right away!" she said, laughing.

"Bye, Raven," I said.

When I hit the top of our stairs, the door to the apartment banged open. I thought maybe it was the Piranhas! But it was Nora.

She ran out and threw her arms around me. "Ace! You're a TV star. You're a movie star. I love you! I love your costume."

"What!"

"We saw you this morning. You were on the *This Morning* show!"

"I thought the TV wasn't working."

"It's fine. A tube had come loose; I fixed it."

"*Everybody saw me?*" I asked, moaning, suddenly looking at her hard. "Hey, Nora! What's wrong with your face?"

"I had my hair done. And Mom let me get into her makeup. Like it?"

She looked like a chimpanzee. Blue eye shadow and ringlets all over her head. "It's wild," I said tactfully.

"Mom gave me the day off; we *both* went to the beauty salon." I moaned again, dreading to see Mom. She was going to give me h—. Nora was smiling toward the doorway. I followed her gaze and saw Mom. With ringlets, too. In a T-shirt. Black with red trim.

"*Ace*," she said shyly. *Not* Horace.

"Oh," I said.

"Couldn't you have told me what you were up to? Didn't you think we might have been proud?"

"What?"

"Oh, not that your dad's not angry that you have gotten so secretive and we—we—wonder what *kind* of people those Falcons really are—"

"I can explain," I said, my mind a blank.

"Well, you'll have to do that later when Dad comes home. He'll expect the honest truth, Ace, and that's what you've got to give him. But Nora and I have a little surprise—come inside the apartment."

The transformation had hit the apartment, too. There were new curtains. "From Bloomies," Mom said. "Vibrant brown." *Brown!* And the table had been moved in front of the windows and there was a spread on it big enough for a Hobart family reunion. Salamis and cheeses and breads and a big chocolate cake right in the middle!

"From Dumas," she said reverently. "Help yourself."

"But why? The place doesn't look half bad. I like your curls, Mom. The curtains—wow!"

"Cake, *Ace?*" Nora, said and burst out laughing. "Mom, I can't get used to it!" she screamed. Mom had gone into the kitchen to get something to drink for all of us. Nora whispered that Mom said we had to call me Ace from now on, since it was my chosen name. "She never wanted to name you Horace anyway. It was Grandma Hobart's idea! How'd you think up *Ace?*" she asked.

"I'm glad Mom doesn't mind it, but what's all the food for?"

"You! She loves you're a star. We're celebrating moving to New York finally."

The phone rang. "I'll get it! I'll get it!" Nora screamed.

"Hello! Hobarts' residence. This is Nora Hobart, Ace's sister. To whom am I speaking?"

It was so embarrassing I had to turn away.

"Ace, do you know a Mr. Stab Evans of the Piranha Company?"

"What!"

She clamped her hand over the mouthpiece. "I think it's a pop record guy. Want me to get rid of him?"

I slid across the floor and grabbed the phone.

"Don't knock me down!" she howled.

"This is Ace," I said into the receiver, trying to sound as tough as Freddy. "Who's this?"

"Mom! He's acting on the phone—come see him," Nora yelled.

A high-pitched voice said, "This is Stab. I got yer friend George here at the Six Hundred and Three playground and he wants you to come and get him." He sounded mean and ugly.

"Is he okay. You do anything to him?"

"Not yet. And we won't if you *do what you're told,* man."

"Okay, what do you want me to do?" I asked. Nora was standing close to me, whispering, "Who is it, Horace—I mean, Ace—what's he want?" I shoved her with my elbow, but she didn't budge.

"Ya listenin'?" Stab said. There was a big pause.

"Yeah! Yeah! What do you want me to do?" I asked.

"Ya listenin'?" he asked again in his high-pitched voice. "Come to School Six Hundred Three."

"Okay, where is it?"

"Duane and Hudson," he said.

"Duane and Hudson? Where are they?" My heart was skipping beats.

"Get off the downtown A train at Chambers, dummy. Wanna speak to George? He's got some instructions for you."

"Yeah, yeah."

"Ace!" George said. "Sorry to bother you like this, but—I need your help."

"Are you okay?" I was so glad to hear his voice.

He didn't answer. "Want me to bring the others, George?"

"No. Come alone, strictly alone. That's what Stab wants, okay? I might not make it if you don't—"

"Okay, okay, don't worry."

"They just want you to come, Ace—they say they want the star."

They, I thought. The phone clicked and George was gone.

"What was it, Ace?" Nora said, finally moving off me.

I blew out a lungful of air. "Listen, get on the phone the minute I leave and call this number." I wrote it on the message pad. "Ask for Freddy. Tell him I've—"

"The one who looks like a movie star?"

"Tell him I've talked to George. I'm going to get him."

Mom had come into the room holding a tray full of glasses and soda bottles. "What did they want with

you? Will you be home for dinner? Dad wants to talk
to you—you can't just go running off whenever you
want to, Horace! You're still a kid, you know!"

"I'll be back!" I said, pulling the patch out of my
pocket, sliding it down over my eye, and zooming out
the door. I felt like Superman leaving the phone booth.

"Hey, that's *my* patch!" Nora screamed after me.
"You give it *back*, Horace!" She was leaning over the
bannister, her voice following me.

I flew down those stairs and out the door, heading
for the nearest subway.

NINETEEN

COMING UP out of the Chambers street station, I looked for Duane Street. The sidewalks in front of the junky old stores were bustling. Just as I dodged two pokey women crossing an intersection ahead of me, my patch broke. It fell off, and by the time I'd rescued it it had been stepped on and mangled. The hole holding the elastic band to the patch was worn through. There wasn't anything to tie it to now.

"Crap!" I muttered. A bus and truck roared by, filling the air with noxious fumes. Two taxis honked. I was still in the middle of the street, my thoughts going wild. How could I beat up Stab with my whole face showing? I stuffed the useless patch in my pocket and decided to turn around and beat it.

But before I'd gone the first cowardly ten feet back home, I tripped on the crummy sidewalk and stumbled into a plate-glass window full of books. My head hit hard. When my eyes opened, Nevada Culhane's latest, *Confessions of a Nervous Detective*, was staring me in the face like a reproach.

It was just what I needed, because I straightened up and started to think like Nevada. One of his mottos is: *Scheme, surprise, and trick. Answers are in front of your nose.* Instead of running like a ninny, I had to concentrate, figure, and plan.

I looked around, taking in the surroundings. What was here? What could help me? Across the street was The Priceless Cheese Store, on the corner a truck that said A NICE JEWISH BOY, MOVERS. In between the cheese store and a cleaners was a tiny bakery. I sniffed and caught its aroma. *Think. Think.*

An idea shot into my head like an arrow.

"Hey!" I called out running through the bakery door. "Got any of those fancy decorated cakes? Like the ones people order for weddings and anniversaries?"

Except for the frizzy-haired woman behind the counter, there was nobody in the store. "Yellow or pink?" she said.

Yellow, I thought, then realized that meant cowardice. "Pink," I said. "Bright pink close to red."

"Pink's pink. How big?"

"How big. Big! What the heck! The biggest in the store." I patted my wallet. It was filled with tens.

"Want something written on it?" she said.

"Can you do it fast?"

"Right away! Here." She slipped a pad under my hand and gave me a pen.

The inscribed cake was twenty-four inches around. It cost a mint! But I paid gladly and ran out the door to the street. It was heavy enough to slow me down.

There was Duane Street.

I looked east and saw an old brick building a block away. I headed for it. Half the side was caved in, revealing three floors of former classrooms, blackboards and all, the floors out, and the bottom filled with trash. So much for teaching, learning, and cheating at Six Hundred Three.

Nobody seemed to be around there, so I whistled. An ear-splitter learned at camp.

Nothing.

I whistled again, standing stock still on the corner, looking six ways around me.

Carefully carrying the cake, which kept shifting heavily in the box, I stepped into the trash-heaped field around the school. Over toward the river the sky was a mean orange and the sun half-drowned in the Hudson. Step, step. Stop and look. How many Piranhas were here, how many in the hospital after the gang war? Did they know the other gangs there the Falcons didn't know? I was sure of it. What were they going to try to do to me, I wondered. I prepared myself for blood and gore, for George with a beaten-up, pulpy face. I pictured him that way so I wouldn't be shocked at anything. I'd be cool in the face of horrors like Nevada; he said it only took practice.

The silence and emptiness were getting me. So I tried crow calling. "*Caw-caw!*" I cried as crows do leaving the nest to forage, their sounds menacing and chilling. It sounded almost right for a Falcon. Step, step—I went toward the building. "*Caw-caw*, George! Piranhas! It's Ace!" The emptiness swallowed the sounds.

I moved across the cluttered field whispering things to myself: *Be cool, think, think, th—*

Suddenly I was grabbed from behind. "Hey!" I yelled, tripping and spinning my head to see who it was. I clutched the cake box; it had almost slipped away. The guy had me pinned so tight I couldn't get free. His face was turned away. No matter—I didn't know him. He was taller than me by a half a foot. *Think, think—*

"Ace Hobart!"

I recognized the high, strangulated tones of Stab. Breathing hard, he was shoving me bodily toward the side of Six Hundred Three.

Think, think, cool, cool. "Present," I said, licking my lips slowly between words, "How are you? Fine, I hope."

He'd pushed me right up to the junky side of the school finally; my knees were turning to jelly. I didn't feel so cool now, if I ever had. I had to force the image of Nevada into my head. I was Nevada. I was invincible. *Oh, boy!*

Stab was talking. "Whatcha got in that snow-colored box, man?" He had his pincers on me, going through the cloth of the Marabunta jacket into my trembling flexed biceps.

"A present for the Piranhas," I said through clenched teeth.

He let out a string of curses. "You can't buy us off with nothin' but money!" he said. We were wading through a ton of trash, heading for the back of the school. There still was *nobody else* around.

I tried being Nevada again. "Nice place, Stab, you call it home?"

He jerked my arms. "Shut yer face or you'll move in here for good!"

I forced a yawn. "How much farther? This little box is heavy!"

"You hold that thing until the Tall One has a chance to see it or your neck is mine!"

A threatener, Nevada Culhane said inside me. Of course, Nevada couldn't feel the dents in my arms.

We got to the back and suddenly I saw the rest of them. Three guys stood around a fire, looking at us, except for one, whose head was invisible in a paper bag.

George?

It was. I recognized the Falcon jacket. His hands were behind him; I don't think he could move them.

"Nice fire! Thanks for inviting me to your jamboree," I said to Stab, licking my lips some more. His tall pals looked mean as the fish they were named after. There wasn't a drop of blood on George, but his shoulders drooped like a roof on the verge of collapse. "George, hi!" I said.

"Shut up, man!" the Piranhas said together. I didn't recognize any of their voices from Saturday. The fringes of panic started to spread and blur the image of Nevada in my mind.

"Hurry up! See what he brought in the box, Helmet!"

"Look out!" the tallest, goose-necked one said. "Put it down over there to open it."

"Don't trust him!" Stab screeched.

"Make him open it hisself, man, I ain't doing it," the other guy said. His red knit hat hugged his head like a helmet, hiding something disgusting—probably the mange. In the fire's glow the whites of his eyes looked lemon yellow.

Stab pushed me over to where the tall guy had put the box, his fingers still piercing my arms.

"Until I see George's face," I said through my teeth, "I'm not opening it."

The guy in the helmet cap pulled the bag off George. "Come out, he wants to see ya, Georgie-Porgie." He was as pale as Swiss cheese. The bright firelight made him blink and shut his eyes. But he wasn't bloody.

"I got your jacket, Ace," he said, still blinking.

"What!" I said.

He turned around so I could see his back. There it was, tied around his wrists. "Hey, you found it!"

"The Piranhas let me know *they* found it and came for me at school this morning. Trouble is they want a reward—to be paid for returning it—and, uh, *Ace!*"

"What?" I said, wondering if they'd be satisfied with the bucks I had left on me.

"We ain't got any *real* money yet, have we?" he said with significance. In spite of Stab boring holes in my arm bones, I caught his message and said, "Right! In fact it took everything I had to cough up the price of this present for the poor Piranhas who are still in the hospital."

George looked puzzled.

"No presents—we want money!" Stab and his pals said.

"If you don't let go, I can't open this box for you,"

I said. The sweat began to coat my forehead. I thought my arms were dead, the circulation permanently disrupted.

"Let him open it," the tall guy said.

Stab loosened his grip and a hundred fiery needles danced down my arms into my numb hands. He shoved me toward the box, which lay in weeds a few feet from the fire.

"If it's firearms or tricks, your buddy's doomed!" said Stab who was now applying his irresistible pressure to George's arms.

"What have you got there, Ace?" George said, looking as doubtful as the rest. I had a sudden urge to throw the cake at all of them and run. They were going to laugh, then kill George and me.

I opened the box. The gang and George waited a beat and then came over to look inside.

Then everybody looked at me and I looked into the box. "A little cheering up for your injured brothers in the hospital from the Falcons."

"It's a cake," the tall guy said.

"For us?" Helmet Cap said. "Probably arsenic."

"Huh!" Stab said when he saw the writing and the sugar roses. "What's it say?"

"I'll read it. 'Get well, feel swell, things aren't the same without you. To the Piranhas from the Falcons.' " Helmet Cap said.

"Well, I'll be!" Stab lifted a rosebud and stuck it in his mouth. "Tastes good."

"Yeah," Helmet Cap said. "But there's only one guy left in the hospital. The others were just in for observation—know what I mean?" he said in a nasty voice.

"Oh! Where are they *now*?" I checked the shadows all around us.

Stab ate another rosebud. "Wait a sec! We're the ones with the questions."

George stiffened. "What d'ya want to know?"

"Saturday night. *Who* were them other guys?" Stab said.

George started to say, "*We* don—"

I interrupted fast. "What do you mean?" I said, suddenly amazed they didn't know either. The three Piranhas looked extremely tense.

"Who were those other gangs near the waterfront? Those two gangs mentioned in the papers?" the tall guy said.

"You mean, they didn't introduce themselves? I told them to," I said, my brain racing.

George looked at me, puzzled, and then a crafty expression came into his eyes. We were on the same wavelength. "Right," he said. "The Piranhas wouldn't know your *pals* from Jersey, would they?"

"Guess not. They don't cross the river much."

"Who! Who were they?" the Piranhas said.

"You know Ace is here from Jersey, don't you? Well, they were the guys he used to run with in Guttenberg. That right, Ace?"

"Only a couple of the gangs," I said. "These were undergrounders from Hackensack. No more than forty guys or so."

"Sheez!" Stab said. The Piranhas looked at him.

"Undergrounders? What's zat?" Helmet Cap said.

"It's *who* the undergrounders got a connection with —*know what I mean*?" George said in a sinister way.

I shook my head in complete agreement. "Don't tell me you never heard of—naw, it's impossible—everybody—"

"Who! Who!" the Piranhas demanded.

"I thought you'd *know* who—he *is* the connection," I said, just as sinister as George, maybe more.

"Who the—" Stab swore.

Think, think. It came to me! "You never heard of Killer Calvin Feckelworth?" I said.

The guys whirled their heads to see which one of them might have a clue. Finally the goose-necked guy said, "Uh—yeah—yeah! Sounds familiar, think I have. Do you know where the Jersey gangs are now?"

"We're in touch at all times," I told them.

Stab was just about to say "How?" when he seemed to think better of it.

"Are they watchin' now?" he asked instead.

"They got weapons?" Helmet Cap asked.

All of a sudden I could tell they were seriously thinking of leaving. But then Stab said, "Wait up! How'd you guys get outta there the other night? We seen ya. We'd followed ya, and then—you disappeared! Now where—where'd ya go?"

"Man, we been trying to tell ya, but ya won't hear," George said. "Ace has got *big gang* connections, the *mob*, the *syndicate*, and not just the national one, the *international* mob. They met us down near the docks and warehouses and then they drove us home in a limousine." He looked straight at me. "Right, Ace?" And then he frowned, I didn't know what that meant.

The Piranhas looked blasted. They shifted their dazzled eyes from George and me to the big pink cake. "Well, heh-heh-heh-heh . . . We sure appreciate your thoughtfulness, and we're gonna take it to the boy in the hospital right now!"

George was sort of staring at me and I winked fast in honor of our victory. He looked at me all the harder.

"About time we was on better terms," Goose Neck said. "We can look out for each other in the Big Apple," he said.

George grinned at him. "All right!" he said.

Stab ran around behind George and untied his hands. He shook out my jacket gingerly and handed it to me. "Hope it's not too wrinkled—we tried to take good care of it," he said, his mouth twitching.

"You'll get the cleaning bill—don't worry!"

"Fine! Fine!" he said.

"Hey!" the tall guy said. "Wanna go to the hospital with us and see the guy still in there?"

"Is it Cannibal?" I asked.

"Cannibal? Naw. Hearse ran over his foot is all. Wasn't broke or nothing. You shoulda seen him, though, blubberin' like a baby. Biggest two-hundert-'n'-eighty-pound boob ya ever seen. Say!" He looked at me sideways. "How'd you know we had a guy named Cannibal?"

I poked my head with a finger. "I gotta sixth sense."

"Oh!" They looked at each other and nodded like they believed it, too. Helmet Cap said, "We can take you to Bellevue to see Turtle—he's in with a broken nose, gotta a tube up there."

George and I started inching toward the street together, begging off with a lot of excuses. We were almost far enough to hightail it out of there when

George stopped short. He looked at me, stunned. "Now I know what it is. Ace! *Your eye!*"

"My eye?" I'd forgotten. "Oh!" Slowly I brought my hands to my face and felt. George and the Piranhas who'd followed us part way stared at me dumbstruck.

"Yeah! I thought so! You had a patch on TV," Stab said.

I felt my cheek, my nose, and then very gently touched the eye that had been covered. *Think. Think. Think.* Nothing came to me. *Think! Think!* I closed my eyes and then opened them. "George," I said. "I can see! I can see!"

"He can see!" Stab said, who'd come very close and was looking intently into my face. "With the both of his eyes!"

"Man, he ain't blind no more!" the tallest one said.

Stab let out a whoop. Helmet Cap said in an awed voice, "It's a miracle! The Falcons have had a miracle!"

George's eyes narrowed.

"Let's get outta here!" I muttered, and we turned and ran to the street.

George speeded ahead of me. "Wait up, don't be mad," I called at the first corner. He was heading for Chambers, half a block in front of me already. "Wait up!" When he got to next corner, he suddenly grabbed at a lamp post and, holding on to it tight, swayed like he was going to pass out.

"What's wrong?" I said, catching up.

He burst out into loud guffaws. He couldn't talk. "You—had—us—fooled—whoo!" he roared. "You— Ha ha ha!"

"I'm sorry, honest! It was an accident. An emergency

situation forced me to wear the patch on the first day of school and then—forces beyond my control . . . Hey! I can explain."

"You had us all fooled—even Raven, man!" He was holding on to the pole like a drunk, swaying back and forth.

"I'm sorr—"

"Every time we got together when you weren't there, we tried to figure out what had happened to your eye." He cackled like a hen. "Oh, sh—" He had the craziest, funniest laugh for a tough guy. It went higher than a goat's, was crazier than a maniac's.

"Hey! I'm really sor—"

"Don't be sorry, man, it's the funniest . . . Ha! Ha!" To hear him laugh set me off. People passing stopped to stare and that just made us laugh harder.

"Hey, George, Killer Calvin Feckelworth never *saw* a gang—I made it all up!" I said roaring.

"I don't think anybody else was there Saturday. They believed the papers, Ace!"

We couldn't stop laughing. It was like an ocean smashing over a dam. Gasping for breath, holding each other up, we stumbled off to the subway.

TWENTY

EVERYBODY WAS huddled on the stoop in front of my house. I could see them when we rounded the corner—Raven in a gold jacket, the Falcons, the Maroons, and Webber, too.

Slick ran toward us, "George, you all right?"

"It's okay, Slick. Okay, really," George said when we got together. "Ace saved me and it was amazing. But first, there's been a miracle. The Falcons have had their first miracle—believe me! Take a look at Ace!"

By then we'd reached the others. Raven put up her hands and covered her eyes. "Ace!" she said behind them.

"What's going on? Where's the patch? Cover your eye—you don't want the public to see that!" Marilyn whispered, sidling up to me.

"His eye!" the Falcons said.

"It looks fine, so what?" said Webber.

George raised his arms like a gospel preacher and said, "He can see! He can see at last!"

"What are you . . . Putting us on?" Freddy said.

J.D. said, "Hey—hey—hey! Something's funny. Freddy, do you smell a rat?" He got up close, followed by Freddy. "Ace, tell the truth, man," he said in a husky voice.

"He fooled us all!" George hollered.

"Nobody fools us, George!" Freddy said, looking genuinely upset. "Nobody fools the Falcons—"

"Except a real true Falcon," said Raven all of a sudden, lowering her hands and starting to laugh.

"Hey, Ace! Yer eye don't look too bad, it really don't—you guys are really rude!" Slick said. "Pay no attention to them. They've been through a strain, that's all. You lost your patch—you can get another one."

"Cut it out, Slick!" Freddy said. "Don't you know it's all right?"

"Oh," Slick said. "Ain't nothin' wrong with his eye?"

"That's right!" everybody said.

"Hey, that's funny!" Slick said, and cleared his throat.

"Hi, everybody! Wouldn't you like to come up to Ace's for some dinner? We're having our first open house since we moved in and we'd like you to come."

I turned around and saw Nora standing in the doorway to the apartment building wearing a big smile and all those funny ringlets.

"Hey, come on up!" I said. "Meet the folks."

"I'm starved!" said J.D., and he led the way for everybody.

Mom and Dad were at the door as soon as we got upstairs and they gave us a big welcome. Pop said,

"Talk to you later, kiddo," in his you're-not-going-to-get-away-with-everything voice, and then ushered everybody in and treated us as good as they treated the Rotary Club when they used to come to parties in Guttenberg.

We ate and played records and Nora danced with Freddy and then shocked everybody by saying to the Falcons, "Tell us some of the bad things you've done. I know you're muggers."

"Well, let's see," said George. "Did you know we once sneaked under the subway turnstile when we didn't have any money and got in free?"

"And we don't ever put money in parking meters," said J.D.

"Why?" said Nora.

"We don't have any cars."

"We steal the racing results out of the trash cans, right?" Raven said.

"And we've definitely been known to mug anybody who mugs us," said Freddy.

"Gee, Ace, I kinda liked the patch," Raven said, squashed in next to me on the couch. I was sitting as close as I could.

"Aww, Raven—" Maybe she wouldn't like me anymore. "I can see you so much better now. Did I ever tell you I like your Hershey kisses eyes and your silky hair?" I whispered.

"You tricker! I guess I don't mind it's gone too much."

"You'll get used to it."

"Promise?"

J.D. said, "He sure pulled the wool over our eyes."

"You mean he pulled the patch," Slick said, and started to giggle.

J.D. let out a hoot. "Give the guy his jacket."

Freddy was carrying a shopping bag and out of it he pulled a beautiful black leather jacket. "Ace's!" he said. "Here, try it on! Ya sure fooled us, Ace."

My mother gasped. "Oh, no! Promise you'll never wear it in Guttenberg!"

Everybody laughed. "Cross my heart," I said. We were all hooting like crows. Or like Falcons.

It was the best time I ever had.

Bound and Gagged took two months to finish. The premiere was on Valentine's Day at Cinema-World II on 42nd Street.

Aunt Betty came, but Jake couldn't make it. The police raided Consolidated Rice Company, Inc., a week after the gang war. Even the funeral parlor wasn't real. Jake's turning state's witness against his pal, Mickey. He says Mickey isn't, and never was, an undertaker. Also, he's promised Aunt Betty that when he gets out of the pen he's giving up his old business associates. He sounded very sincere. I believe him.

Webber's writing a book about his experiences as a desk clerk and the Maroons are back in L.A. negotiating another film. A multimillion-dollar extravaganza this time, featuring a shipwreck and some singing nuns who keep everybody's spirits up on the lifeboats. The reviews of our film ranged from "abominable" to "worst movie ever," but it's a big hit at the box office.

Just as Marilyn said, every kid in America loved it.

P.S. I found out why Slick has letters on his fingers. He cheats on tests.

About the Authors

Barbara Beasley Murphy is the author of *Thor Heyerdahl and the Reed Boat Ra* (with Norman Baker) and *No Place to Run*. She lives in New Rochelle, New York.

Judie Wolkoff is the author of *Wally* and *Where the Elf King Sings*. She lives in Chappaqua, New York.

S. E. HINTON